*To WHITNEY —*

# THE PRICE OF LIFE

*FROM YOUR AGGIE BROTHER...*

# GREG McCARTHY

Otherworld Publications, LLC

Louisville, Kentucky

Otherworld Publications, LLC
4949 Old Brownsboro Rd. Suite 113
Louisville, Kentucky 40222
www.otherworldpublications.com

Interior design and typesetting by Lynn Calvert
Cover design by JEDesign
Cover and interior design Copyright © 2010 Otherworld
Publications, LLC

This is a work of fiction. Names, characters, places, and incidents either are the product of the author's imagination or are used fictitiously, and any resemblance to actual persons, living or dead, business establishments, events, or locales, is entirely coincidental.

Author Photo used with permission by Susan Blair Photography

Printed in the United States of America

Paperback     ISBN10: 0-9826494-5-2
              ISBN13: 978-0-9826494-5-9
Hard Cover    ISBN10: 0-9826494-4-4
              ISBN13: 978-0-9826494-4-2
Library of Congress Control Number:  2010922826

*To my family. You are everything to me.*

# AUTHOR'S NOTE

In early 2003, the Texas legislature passed a law affecting lawsuits against healthcare providers representing the culmination of nearly twenty years of effort in tort reform. The law, which applies only to healthcare providers and not to any other class of citizens, imposes tougher standards for claims against doctors and hospitals, setting out a minefield of hazards for lawyers representing victims in these cases. Most lawyers who handle these cases regularly have no philosophical difficulty with establishing the merits of their case at an early juncture.

On the issue of damages, however, the law does not discriminate between clearly meritorious cases and those which could rightly be characterized as frivolous. There is no limit on recovery of "economic" damages such as lost earnings or medical expenses, but even in cases in which liability is crystal clear, there is a cap on recovery of "non-economic" damages of $250,000. These damages have been recognized for more than 100 years of Texas jurisprudence for physical impairment, pain and mental anguish, disfigurement, and loss of consortium for the death of a family member. The practical effect of this law is that a case involving millions in medical expenses and loss of income might still be viable, but the death of a child, a non-working wife, or an elderly parent will almost never result in a recovery of more than $250,000.

In September 2003, the voters of Texas went to the polls and considered an amendment to the Texas Constitution that essentially made the new law immune to attack in the courts of our state. The measure passed by a razor-thin margin.

# PROLOGUE

Eight-year-old Jennifer Haller lay motionless on the hospital bed, her head slightly higher than her feet. Her eyelids were closed, hiding what once was a pair of eyes more blue than the deepest sea. Even when open, those eyes had lost their sparkle, and it wouldn't return. A rhythmic monotone filled the room, reporting that the patient was still alive, if only clinically so.

Julie Haller sat in a straight-backed chair next to her daughter's bed, holding Jennifer's hand as she had done for the past two days. She'd rarely left the bedside, refusing food and sleep. She wanted to be there when Jennifer woke up. She needed to be there if she didn't. Julie caressed her daughter's bare scalp with her free hand, taking care not to rub too hard on the skin still healing from radiation burns. Julie's mind still registered the feel of her daughter's hair in her hand. The hair was once silky and thick, but fell out by the handful as radiation and chemotherapy progressed. As she gently moved her hand, she spoke in muted tones to Jennifer, telling her daughter she was loved and trying desperately to pierce the wall the coma had built between them.

"Are you sure you don't want anything to eat, Mrs. Haller?" asked the nurse, poking her head into the doorway.

"No, thank you," Julie replied without turning around. It was close to noon, but Julie honestly didn't know the time, nor did she care.

"Captain Haller is here," the nurse said. "I'm not supposed to let both of you in here at the same time."

Julie shot her a glare and drew a breath, but the nurse raised both hands in surrender.

"I said I'm not supposed to," said the nurse, patting Julie on the shoulder. "We'll be right back."

Julie nodded, turning back to her daughter.

The nurse returned shortly, pushing the wheelchair bearing Ed Haller, his left foot resting on the stirrup and his right pant leg tied at the stump of his right leg.

"Any change?" Haller asked.

"Not yet. I keep talking to her, but not yet."

"Want me to take over?"

"No, Ed, you should get some rest yourself."

"I've had enough rest, and you've been here two days without leaving. Really, honey, let me stay with her." He reached out and massaged the back of Julie's neck with his hand. She didn't seem to notice.

"You can stay if you want," Julie said. "I'm not leaving."

Outside, a soft rain had fallen all morning, and low dark clouds lingered, keeping the sun at bay. Even in the dimly lit room, the pain and exhaustion etched into Julie's face was plain to see. She kept her gaze on Jennifer, ravaged by cancer and by treatment worse than the disease itself. Haller longed to hold his daughter, comfort her, carry her from this horror to a time and place where she was happy and healthy once more. He wanted this more than anything, but he knew it couldn't happen.

Haller maneuvered his wheelchair next to Julie's bedside seat. She inched over to make room, and Haller took his wife's hand, which in turn held his daughter's hand, into his own. They tended Jennifer for nearly three hours, softly stroking her head and her hand, Julie occasionally whispering to her little girl as the constant beep of the monitor kept time like a metronome.

The rhythm grew slower over time and became a continuous tone just before four o'clock in the afternoon.

Julie leaned into the bed and kissed Jennifer's forehead, squeezing her eyes shut in an effort to make it all go away, to wake up from the nightmare that had become her life. When she opened them, the reality struck her again.

Ed Haller still held Jennifer's hand. He waited as his wife hovered over Jennifer, speaking too softly to hear. Finally, Julie turned to her husband. Their eyes met, and she could contain her agony no longer. She fell into his lap and disintegrated into tears, the sobs amplifying as they rose, racking her body in pain to match the anguish of her soul.

As he quietly held his wife in his arms, Ed Haller didn't cry. His eyes narrowed to slits and his jaw tightened, but otherwise there was no outward sign of the fury within.

# CHAPTER 1

Captain Ed Haller, USMC, arrived with his wife at Grant Mercer's office about fifteen minutes early. He was, after all, a Marine officer, and punctuality was a trait that came naturally. Growing up on a working ranch in south Texas, eldest of three sons, Haller had risen early and worked hard his entire life.

Grant came around the corner and winced ever so slightly at the sight of the thin titanium tube between Haller's sock and pant leg. He recovered his composure quickly, but Haller noticed the momentary change in facial expression. Haller stood and introduced himself, then his wife.

"Nice to meet you both," Grant said as he stuck out his hand. "Why don't we sit in the conference room? The view is pretty good, and nobody's using it today. Would you like something to drink?"

"Your receptionist already offered, thank you." Haller took Grant in a polite but extraordinarily powerful handshake. Grant cringed, but refused to rub the wounded paw.

They sat at a large oak table in the center of the room, with Grant in an oversized armchair at the head of the table and the Hallers across the corner. Haller's steely blue eyes scanned Grant quickly before a friendly smile returned to the Marine's face.

"I'd like to get right to it, if you don't mind," said Haller.

Grant gave a slight nod as he started making notes on a fresh yellow pad.

"I got a call while I was still in Iraq," Haller began. "It was about eight months ago. Julie called on a Wednesday evening. Right away, I knew something wasn't right. You have to remember; we don't get many calls over there. With email available to us, we get to communicate pretty much every day, but the phone is still something they keep for special occasions. My son, Bradley, had his birthday last fall, and my daughter, Jennifer, had turned eight about six months before. Jen had been sick for a little while and was complaining more and more about pain in her head. So like I said, I knew something was up.

"Anyway, Julie said Jen had some tests done, and they found a tumor in her head. She said the only way they could take it out was with a laser procedure, but only two places in the world had the laser. I tried to get her to slow down and explain, but she was crying and the telephone connection was in and out, and I barely heard her say our insurance plan wouldn't pay for the procedure because it's experimental. Then she said the doctor told her the tumor would have been visible on a CT scan if they'd taken one a year ago when Jennifer started complaining about the headaches. Doctor said it could have easily been removed back then.

"With all the time gone by and the growth of the tumor, though, they gave Jen only a twenty percent chance to survive. The experimental procedure would have cured her, but all we could get the insurance company to pay for was chemo and radiation." Haller drew a tortured breath, let it out in a long, painful exhale, and continued.

"Jennifer lost her hair, about fifteen pounds, and all her energy. I marveled every day at my daughter's fight and her will to live. I don't think I could be as strong as she was."

Grant cast a quick glance at the titanium prosthesis where Haller's right leg should have been. "I'm not sure I can agree," he said. "That doesn't look like something too easy to recover from."

"This is nothing," replied Haller calmly. "I disconnected from that phone call with Julie and went out on patrol about two hours later. Unfortunately for me, I ran into an Iraqi IED about an hour after that."

"IED," Grant asked.

"The Improvised Explosive Device," Haller said in a detached tone, "is pure evil from the twisted minds of men at war. Some might say it's the cluster bomb, the antipersonnel mine, or the fully automatic assault rifle. But for pure terror of the unknown and unseen, my money's on the IED."

Haller spent a few minutes explaining the mayhem to Grant. As the name implies, the IED is entirely improvised from whatever happens to be on hand. Pipes, metal containers, plastic boxes, gas tanks, and animal entrails have been used at one time or the other as the housing for the device. Explosives of all kinds, from C-4 to nitrogen fertilizer to TNT, provide the force.

"Whoever makes the bomb sets it out on a road, street, or open field and remains close by, usually within a hundred yards, to ensure adequate visibility of the package. They mostly use cell phones as the detonation trigger. It's a simple matter of waiting."

Around Baghdad and other Iraqi cities in time of urban warfare, rubbish and debris lay everywhere. Burned out vehicles, household garbage, dead and dying animals, and the remainder of the flotsam and jetsam of war litters every street, road, and highway. When the patrols of Marines and US Army soldiers canvass the streets to maintain or restore order, they travel on foot, in Humvees, and in armored personnel carriers. Budget restrictions crimp the supply of

APC's and Hummers, and far too often the majority of Marines walk or ride in vehicles with little or no protection. Together with the shortage of protective vests and the inferior quality of the vests available to them, American soldiers become easy targets.

Haller paused a moment. "As a patrol approaches the IED, the triggerman keeps watch, waiting to take down the greatest number of infidels in a single attack. Most don't even engage the detonator at the best time. Not that it matters.

"We were out on patrol in Tikrit," Haller said. "We completed a good sweep about a week before and had cleared out all the insurgents we knew about. The problem is, whenever you kill or take out one, two more come in behind them to claim the territory. At first, we figured that process took about a month. Then it became three weeks. I found out the hard way the transition time was down to about a week, sometimes less.

"As we headed down this one street, we saw a wrecked Toyota pickup truck with a camper shell on the shoulder of the road. The insurgents use these vehicles as half-assed machine gun nests, so we always need to be sure they're actually empty. Protocol says all the men should be in a reinforced Hummer or an APC, but the truth is the open Humvees with the armor up around the front and sides will be fine if there really is an AK-47 or two in that vehicle.

"It was obvious to all of us there was nobody inside the truck. I jumped down with my lieutenant about twenty-five yards away, and we started walking toward the truck, him a little in front of me. Nobody could tell me to get my ass back in the Hummer, but our driver, a lance corporal from Nebraska, told me he wished I'd do just that.

"As I turned around to tell him we're okay, the IED went off. Lt. Schaeffer had just crossed in front of me, so he took the brunt of the detonation and nearly all of the shrapnel right to the front of him. The Kevlar vest was shredded, but the injuries to his head were too much anyway. I don't think he knew what hit him. I hope not."

Haller blinked several times, and his voice trembled, but he continued.

"The force was just unreal. The two guys on the passenger side had cuts from the glass, and the one in the front seat lost the vision in his right eye. I was thrown into the side of the Hummer, and all the glass was blown out of the vehicle. I remember being foggy for awhile, and the guys told me later I was unconscious for about ten minutes.

When I came to, I tried to get up, but it felt like I was swimming in a pool of Jell-O. My legs wouldn't work. My arms wouldn't work. I could see, but everything was cloudy and smoky, and I had a hard time recognizing the things around me. Then I noticed there was somebody right in front of me, telling me to be still and messing around with my leg. Except when I looked, I had no leg. It was just gone. I saw blood, and flesh, and bone, but there was nothing from the knee down.

"I remember being in a helicopter, then on an airplane, but the next time I was conscious awhile was in a hospital at Ramstein Air Force Base in Germany. They told me my leg was gone, but I'd survive. The vest from Julie's parents probably saved my life.

"The next day, Julie arrived in Germany. It was great to see her, but when I found out what had been happening back home, the nightmare started for real."

# CHAPTER 2

"For the first few days in the hospital," Haller continued, "I was in and out of consciousness, sleeping quite a bit. The doctors wanted me calm. Julie kept saying she was just there for me. Her parents were keeping the kids, she said, and they were already planning to spend a couple of weeks together anyway. But the more I talked to Julie, the more I could tell something was bothering her.

"Finally, she told me Jennifer had taken a turn for the worse. The chemo wasn't working, and it was making her sicker than ever. Plus, they found two spots in her lungs and one in her bones where the cancer had spread."

Grant was all too familiar with metastasis of tumors from handling several similar cases. Most often, detection of tumors in another area of the body was a harbinger of disaster, since it usually took a while for the cancer to grow, travel elsewhere, and set up camp. It was definitely not a good sign.

Haller reached into the pocket of his shirt and withdrew a wallet-sized photograph, placing it carefully on the table in front of Grant. It showed a young girl with gentle waves of shiny blonde locks cascading down the sides of her face to her delicate shoulders. Soft, freshly scrubbed skin set off eyes of cerulean blue and a bright, toothy grin.

"I don't know how eight years went by so fast," said Haller sadly. "To me, it seems like yesterday we brought her home from the hospital. She was so tiny." Haller's voice trailed off as he turned his gaze out the window. Beside him, Julie stared blankly at the table.

"Jennifer was just a great kid," Haller whispered. He held the photograph tenderly in his fingers, rubbing the corners and occasionally passing his fingertips across the face of his daughter. "I guess everyone thinks that about their own kids, huh?"

Grant smiled and nodded.

"She was at the perfect age. Still sweet to her mother, still thought we hung the moon. She hadn't been around other kids enough to figure out we're squares, and like bad music, and all the other stuff she would have learned in junior high. She'd always run up to me, jump in my arms, and give me a big kiss. Makes you forget about the bad day at the office, you know?"

Again, Grant nodded kindly. His daughters had been the same when they were little.

Haller drew a deep breath, seemingly collecting all the pain in his body and his heart into one agonizing, palpable knot in his chest, and pressed ahead. "Even after I came back home, I couldn't be there as much as I should have, dealing with this." He tapped his prosthetic leg, a hollow ring coming from beneath the table. "Most of it fell to Julie, and she was trying to help me at the same time. Jennifer made it another six weeks. She fought hard every day, and never gave up, even at the end. My daughter died eleven days short of her ninth birthday."

Grant stayed quiet for awhile. He'd seen too many mothers and fathers who had lost children. He usually found they needed a bit of silence from time to time. When it seemed clear that Haller had come to the end of the story, Grant spoke.

"When did Jennifer die?"

"Almost five months ago." said Haller.

"How are you doing since then?"

"Julie's taken it real hard," Haller responded, taking his wife's hand. "She cried constantly for weeks, and still cries three or four times a day. She's been seeing a therapist, and says that helps."

"How about you?" Grant asked, knowing that Haller would prefer to avoid the question.

"I've been a little busy myself," Haller answered. When I got back stateside I had to spend a lot of my time getting my prosthesis squared away. Since we lost Jen, it just seems like everything takes more and more effort. But I've been getting better the last few weeks." Haller folded his hands in his lap and gave a barely perceptible nod, signaling the end of the discussion of his feelings, at least for the time being.

"Tell me what I can do for you," said Grant.

"Mr. Turner said you might be able to help us with a lawsuit," Haller said calmly.

"Well, I certainly appreciate his confidence," said Grant, "but I hope he had a talk with you about the problems these days with medical malpractice cases."

Julie sat up, staring at Grant. "What problems? I hear all the time about people who sue doctors and hospitals over nothing and collect millions of dollars."

"Mr. Turner didn't tell us about any problems," agreed Haller.

Grant swore under his breath. "First of all, the stories in the press about exorbitant recoveries in frivolous cases are the exception, not the rule. For every case where a minor injury turns into millions, there are dozens where the doctor committed malpractice, but the jury disagreed and the plaintiffs were sent home with nothing.

"Most often, stories about huge jury awards are published immediately after the jury verdict, but they're not newsworthy when the judge reduces the award or an appeals court overturns the verdict a couple years later. You remember the coffee case in New Mexico a few years back?"

"Sure," Haller said. "Old lady didn't know coffee was hot, spilled it on her leg, and got three million bucks. Thanks to her, we have warnings on Starbucks cups to tell us coffee's hot."

"That's the short version," Grant replied. "What most people don't know is that the old lady had third degree burns to her groin and needed skin grafts. They also don't know that the restaurant chain tested the coffee temperatures and knew they were serving it about twenty-five degrees hotter than the highest safe temperature. They did that because their tests showed they could sell more coffee that way."

"You're joking," said Julie.

"It's no joke," Grant said. "The restaurant's accountant testified that these people were 'statistically insignificant.' The jury was incensed, but they actually awarded a relatively small amount of punitive damages when they decided on two million. That was one day of coffee sales revenue for the company."

"One day?" Julie asked.

"Just one day," said Grant with a nod. "Despite all the evidence, the judge decided the jury had disregarded the evidence, and he cut the award down to $750,000. The plaintiffs settled the case six months later for $450,000. That was the same number they demanded before they filed the lawsuit."

The Hallers looked at each other in disbelief. "You said there were problems with medical malpractice cases," Julie said. "That coffee wasn't prescribed by a doctor."

"True," Grant agreed. "But the coffee case had a point. Verdicts against worldwide corporations are one thing. Jurors don't like to think that a doctor in their town makes mistakes, or the hospital where they take their kids to the emergency room isn't up to snuff. Still, that's not the worst of it."

Julie leaned forward. "What's the worst of it?"

"In medical malpractice cases, we have to file a report from a qualified expert detailing our case. That has to be filed shortly after the lawsuit itself. Those rules have been in place for quite a while, but the legislature keeps messing around with those laws.

"Not long ago, they put the finishing touches on their work. The new law makes it harder to file a case at all, because it puts a cap on what you can recover."

"What kind of cap?" Julie asked.

"In these cases," Grant said, "You can recover your medical expenses and your lost earnings in full, but non-economic damages are limited to $250,000."

"What do you mean, non-economic damages?" Haller asked with a scowl.

"I mean all those things that aren't about money. Pain and suffering, mental anguish, and the fact that you've lost your child." Grant sat still, wondering what question might come next.

Haller leaned forward, his voice rising and his body becoming suddenly tense. "You're telling me the government decided my daughter's life is worth only $250,000? That's disgusting."

"I agree," Grant said. "But that's how it is. And it gets worse. Because these cases have a ceiling, insurance companies are in absolutely no hurry to settle. They'll just wait for us to jump through all the hoops, spend all the money, and endure the pain of a lawsuit. If we can do all that for two or three years and the jury sides with us, they'll cut us a check.

"You need to know another thing. Our firm gets forty percent of the recovery for our fee. In addition to that, we get paid back for the money we spend on your case. That can easily get to forty or fifty grand. That means if we get paid two-fifty for the case, and we spend fifty to get there, you wind up with a hundred, which is the same as our fee. And you're the people who lost your daughter."

Haller hesitated for an instant, then sat forward and stared at Grant. The intensity made Grant squirm in his chair.

"Let me tell you something, Mr. Mercer. That sucks. You say if I die because a truck runs over me, the case is worth millions. But if my eight-year-old daughter dies because a doctor didn't order a goddamned X-ray, the most he has to pay is a quarter of a million? That doesn't seem like it would be worth the money or the trouble, for you or for us."

Haller's glare burned more brightly for a split second. Grant swore he saw the Marine's sea-blue eyes turn black, revealing for just a moment the depth of his pain.

"But here's the thing," Haller said. "I don't give a rat's ass about the money. If I had millions and could spend it to get my daughter back, I'd do it in a minute. I just can't let them kill her and sit by doing nothing. You asked what you can do for me. You can take our case.

"Whatever it takes, however long it takes, I have to do this for my family. I have to stand up for my daughter. If I don't do that, who will?"

Haller's last question hit Grant like a sledgehammer. When he walked into the meeting, he'd fully intended to spend thirty minutes with the clients, let them know of the difficulties of medical malpractice litigation, and politely decline the case. Grant's felt his stomach sink. He was embarrassed that he could be such a coward.

During his days as a solo, he'd occasionally been dead broke and frighteningly deep into his personal line of credit, yet he'd been proud of his career. Even in the toughest cases, with the most complex and confusing medical issues, he was always convinced that his cases had merit, that his clients were worthy of his toil and dedication.

Grant was mindful that he practiced his profession in a system created to put an end to pistols at dawn as the favored method of settling differences between citizens. The lawmakers had done everything possible to kill off any chance for a citizen to seek justice for medical malpractice, but they hadn't killed it entirely. Recovery could still be had, even if relatively small, and it was still the only way for people to seek compensation for a wrong done to them. It was up to him, and other lawyers with his skills and experience, to help these people.

Looking at the Marine sitting across from him, Grant felt painfully guilty for doubting his own resolve. Here was a man who'd fought for his country, and had probably done so without questioning the propriety of the war. He simply did his duty, without complaint, and paid a horrible price. Grant's admiration for Haller gave him a sudden rush of confidence, of righteousness, of desire to help this man and his family. Haller had fought for him; it was time to return the favor.

"Captain and Mrs. Haller, I'd be honored to take your case. I just need you to understand the difficulties we face. If I'm going to be your lawyer, I'll have two jobs. First, I'll be your advocate. When I'm talking to our opponent or the jury, I'll tell them all the best things about our case and minimize anything I see as a weakness.

"My second job is to be your counselor, which means that when we're talking alone, I have to tell you honestly about the tough parts of your case, and maybe even tell you that it's not strong enough to go on. If I don't do that, I'm not doing my job."

"No problem, Mr. Mercer," said Haller. "Just keep doing your job, and everything will be just fine."

# CHAPTER 3

It was brutally hot; the kind of hot that makes asphalt shimmer like a mirage no matter how you tilt your head. Grant's white oxford, so crisp that morning, now stuck to his body like a second skin. Untucked, the perfectly ironed fabric moved as he paced, a soft scratching sound emanating from him as the starch made contact with the razor sharp creases of his trousers. He glanced up expectantly as he heard a soft click near the front of the courtroom, grinding to a halt as he turned to the judge's door near the ornately carved oaken bench. The boyish judge, fifteen years younger than Grant himself, nursed a drink that might have been iced tea. The coloring was off, though, and the relaxed expression on the judge's face made Grant wonder if perhaps a shot of whiskey had made its way into the glass. Grant eyed him cautiously, but the judge merely offered him an apologetic shake of his head.

"Sorry, no verdict. The jury's asked to have dinner brought in. How about some barbecue?"

Grant didn't bother to answer as he let his breath escape and resumed his incessant pacing. His legal assistant, sitting barefooted in the front row of the court gallery, offered the judge a faint smile in response. "Thank you, but I think we're fine."

The judge scanned the courtroom. "Where's Mrs. Middleton?"

"She went home," Leslie said. "She's eighty-four, and these benches aren't the best thing for her back."

"They're probably no better on yours," the judge said before retreating to his office.

Grant sank into the chair beside her. "You don't have to stay, Leslie. Why don't you head on back or go get something to eat? We've been waiting nine hours already."

"Nine hours and twelve minutes," she corrected without bothering to answer his offer of freedom. He hadn't really expected her to go anywhere. She and his co-counsel, Chris Turner, had made it quite clear they would be sitting here next week if that's how long it took the central Texas jury to return their verdict.

"Where's Chris?"

"Sleeping with the enemy."

Leslie twisted her head toward the doorway where the hospital's executives and their lawyers fouled the air. Their raucous laughter grated on Grant, particularly this evening. He wasn't sure if it was the tension of waiting on the verdict, the ancient and useless air conditioning in the courtroom, or his lack of sleep, but their cavalier attitude about the trial caused irrational anger to rise from the pit of his stomach.

"Let's get out of here," he grumbled, reaching down to toss Leslie her shoes. "And you get to fetch Chris."

Grant stepped out into the sweltering heat ahead of his little entourage, sucking in a breath of stagnant evening air. Sliding his hands into his pockets, he led them to the café that had become their second home for the past two weeks.

"How do you feel, boss?" asked Leslie.

"Old," Grant replied.

"At least you're getting skinny," she said. "How much weight have you lost?"

GREG McCARTHY

"About fifteen, I guess." Grant shrugged. "My hair's getting gray, too."

"There's not enough to notice." Leslie punched his arm playfully. "Actually, it makes you look distinguished."

Chris Turner broke in. "I'd say it's more like extinguished."

"Laugh it up now, pal," Grant said. "When you're forty-seven and jaded you'll know how I feel."

Chris held the café door open for Leslie, then ushered Grant through the door with a ceremonious wave. "Age before beauty."

Grant was too fatigued to think of a witty retort.

"Teas all around?" The waitress nodded without waiting for an answer and waved them to their usual table in the corner.

"What do you think?" Chris asked with enthusiasm Grant could only envy.

The question hung in the air until the waitress delivered three tall, sweating glasses of dark liquid, each with a wedge of lemon hanging on the rim. Grant longed for a stronger beverage, maybe a nice Scotch or a Crown and Seven, anything that would slow his mind and dull the pain. Once the trial was officially over, he could indulge. For now, Grant took a gigantic gulp of tea as he leaned back in his chair.

"I never know until I hear it from them," Grant said, "but I have a good feeling about this group. They listened. They connected. I even had a few of them nodding at me during my closing."

"As hot as it was in the courtroom, they might have just been taking a nap," Leslie countered, always quick with the needle.

"Thanks." he offered her a sideways grin. "Good to know you're as confident in me as ever."

"Any time."

16

"I'm not sure," Chris said. "I can see them buying that crap about sudden cardiac death from the hospital's experts. It's easy when you don't have the burden of proof."

"Of course it's easy," Grant said. "But when a seventy-six-year-old man goes into the hospital for knee replacement and comes out of surgery with no complications, he shouldn't die the same night. Those nurses didn't follow orders."

"You don't have to sell me," said Chris. "I thought your argument to the jury was great. You sold them."

"Thanks," Grant mumbled. "We'll see soon enough."

"Hey, Chris." Leslie broke in. "What were you doing with those creeps anyway?"

Chris seemed to come alive at her question and began talking at a furious speed. It took a moment for Grant's sleep-deprived brain to catch up with what Chris was telling them.

"They were talking about the Haller case?" Grant hissed.

"They had to be. Eight-year-old girl. Dad's a Marine. It had to be our case."

"Jennifer Haller wasn't in their hospital," Grant said. "How did they know about the case?"

"Lawyers talk, Grant," Leslie added. "You know that."

Grant stared at Chris. "I don't want to know about it. And I damn sure hope you didn't say anything to them."

Chris shook his head. "No way."

"Keep it that way," Grant said. "I'm not sure yet whether I'm keeping the case."

"Come on, man," Chris said. "It's a great case. They're great clients. We're going to kick some ass on that case."

"Absolutely," Grant said sarcastically. "We'll kick some ass. Can we drop it now? I'm tired."

Grant took another long gulp of his tea. He hated letting people down, but he figured remaining quiet and letting Chris chalk it up to exhaustion was better than telling him the truth. He just felt beaten. Not just by the years spent on this case, but by his life in general.

His sense of obligation was suddenly as suffocating as the Texas heat. His wife and family depended on him to provide for their livelihood. His clients, including the widow waiting patiently at home for the jury's verdict, placed their trust and their future in his hands. The pressure grew with each case, each client, and each passing year, until Grant had begun to wonder whether he could withstand it any longer.

"Grant." Leslie tugged on his arm to grab his attention. She nodded toward the courthouse where the bailiff's back was just visible re-entering the courthouse. "We've got a verdict."

# CHAPTER 4

Grant Mercer was back to the grind. He sat behind his desk at five-thirty on a summer afternoon trying to will another half hour of work from his exhausted mind and body.

Chris Turner poked his head in the door. "Isn't it time for you to go home?"

Grant looked up, startled. "Security sucks in this building. What are you doing here?"

"Just left a hearing," Chris said. "Any news on the Haller case?"

Grant waved at his desk, where files sat in stacks from one end to the other. "You're worse than the clients, Chris. I've been stuck with this crap since we finished the trial."

Chris frowned. "Try to contain your enthusiasm."

"Sorry," Grant said. "I'm just bushed. The Middleton case still bothers me."

"It's been two weeks," Chris said. "You usually bounce back better than that."

"Yeah," said Grant. "Middleton's different. I still can't figure out how the jury was so badly misled."

"We've seen that before, Grant," Chris said. "Any case can be lost, especially medical malpractice cases."

"That was no help when I had to explain to my partner how we lost seventy thousand dollars in expenses and didn't earn a fee."

Chris shrugged. "At least you're free to do status reports for insurance adjusters."

"You're a funny guy," Grant said. "I haven't slept more than a couple hours in two weeks. When I do, I dream about the trial."

"That sounds cool," Chris said with a smile.

Grant sat silently for a moment. "I made a serious vocational error. I should be mowing lawns for a living."

Chris sighed. "You're good at what you do, Grant. You have what everybody else wants. Look at your family. Beautiful wife and two beautiful kids. Thank God the kids look like their mom."

"Amen to that," said Grant.

"Hell, I want to be you when I grow up."

"Thanks, Chris. Maybe you should take the Haller case."

"You're the trial lawyer, man." Chris looked at Grant. "That's a good case. You should keep it. It's the right thing to do."

"The right thing?" Grant asked. "I know we used to think the right thing was important. We thought we'd represent clients who loved us and do great things for them. It doesn't work that way, Chris. The right thing doesn't exist."

"What happened to my friend the idealist?" Chris asked.

"I haven't been an idealist for twenty years."

Turner shook his head. "You're wrong there. You're a disappointed idealist. That means you're a cynic."

"Whatever name you want," said Grant. "It's all the same."

Chris stood and walked to the window, his back to his friend. "I know it hasn't been easy for you, working for Montgomery's insurance clients. You've always hated that work."

"It eats at my soul," Grant said.

"I understand." Chris nodded. "But you don't have to do it all the time. You've got your own clients, doing the Lord's work. You've won your share."

"The politicians are taking that away, Chris."

"They sure are, but even the politicians can't take everything away," Chris said. "Med mal cases aren't what they used to be, but this is a good case."

"No such thing as a good med mal case, Chris." Grant fell into his chair. "I don't know if I have the strength to do this."

"Then why didn't you just tell them no?" Chris turned to face Grant. "Why make them wait? Call them and tell them you're not going to represent them. Tell them you want no part of working for people like them. Tell them you'd rather work for insurance companies."

Grant sat in stunned silence. Chris was right. He couldn't stand the thought of subsisting on the status reports and drudgery of an insurance defense practice. "I'm keeping their case," Grant said. "I just hope I have enough left to survive the fight."

# CHAPTER 5

After nearly a month catching up on the rest of his cases, Grant set aside the time to focus on the Haller case. His clients had some medical records, but by no means all of them. It took three weeks to gather the paper, and his next task was to hire qualified experts to look at them. Within four months of filing suit, Grant would need to supply a report stating clearly how the doctors had been negligent in their treatment of Jennifer Haller and describing how the negligence had directly caused her death.

Grant usually looked out of state to find an expert willing to review cases and testify against doctors in Texas. He understood it would be awkward at best, and professional suicide at worst, to offer expert testimony against another local doctor. As a result, Grant's list was heavily populated with doctors from both coasts, the upper Midwest, and the Southeast. He tried to look on the bright side and considered these cases opportunities to see other parts of the country.

For the Haller case, Grant enlisted the help of Fredrick Howard, M.D., a pediatric neurologist and professor at the University of Washington Medical Center in Seattle. After a couple of phone calls, Grant sent the records to Dr. Howard, along with a check for three thousand dollars, representing an advance to Dr. Howard for six hours' work at his usual rate of five hundred dollars an hour. Though most of his friends were surprised to hear it, Grant considered this rate to be exceptionally reasonable, even low. Two weeks after receiving the records, Dr. Howard had completed his review and called Grant to discuss the case.

"This looks like a pretty clear case to me, Grant. Seven-year-old children don't typically complain of headaches on a daily basis, and they usually don't have them in the morning. Nausea and vomiting are also unusual when they accompany headaches for an extended period. There's no question in my mind that Dr. Purser should have ordered the CT scan on her first visit."

"Fine," Grant countered, "but can you say it made a difference?"

"I'm sure it did," Howard replied. "But I don't think I'm going to be allowed to offer that testimony, am I?"

"You're right," Grant said. "For that, we need a surgeon, don't we?"

"We do indeed. What about Dr. Lester down at UCLA? We've worked cases together for you, if I recall correctly."

"I had in mind putting in a call to Richard Perkins instead," Grant said.

"Rick's good at what he does, but he's in San Antonio, and your case is in Fort Worth. Is he willing to testify against other Texas docs?"

"I've taken his deposition six times," Grant said. "Every time he says he's willing to look at cases for plaintiffs' lawyers, but nobody ever asks him."

Perkins would bring a whole new dimension to the case, and Grant knew it. He'd been doing surgery on the brain, including tumors, for more than twenty-five years. Perkins had pioneered the use of the laser scalpel in surgical treatment of brain tumors. This work was still underway, and the use of the laser hadn't been approved for that particular use, so it remained an experimental procedure.

"Let me know if you need any help getting him to play on our team," said Howard. "In the meantime, get busy drafting a report."

Dr. Perkins was a surprisingly easy sell. Grant reminded him of their conversations about working for a plaintiff's lawyer, and Perkins agreed on the spot. The only sticking point was his fee, which was nine hundred dollars an hour, much closer to the usual rate charged by medical experts in lawsuits. Grant tried valiantly to get Perkins to reduce the fee. His clients, whose daughter had died and one of whom was battling his own medical issues, would ultimately have to pay for it.

None of this swayed Perkins, who explained his exorbitant rates as his rationalization for getting into the mud pile of litigation and playing with the swine inhabiting the mud pile. Grant relented and sent a stack of medical records more than a foot thick to the good doctor, along with a retainer check for six thousand dollars. He'd been the attorney for Ed and Julie Haller for less than two months and had already spent more than ten thousand dollars on their case. Just the tip of the iceberg, Grant figured.

# CHAPTER 6

William O. Sellett, Esquire, reclined in his black leather chair, stretching his long legs to let his feet rest on the corner of his Chippendale desk. Rocking the crystal highball in his hand, he watched absently as the ice cubes swirled around the edges, tinkling softly against the hand-made glass. Before the chill could settle in, Sellett took a healthy sip of the eighteen-year-old Macallan single malt scotch his secretary had poured for him. From his office high atop the gleaming new Frost Bank building in downtown Austin, Sellett had the most coveted view in the city. On sunny afternoons, the shimmering waters of Town Lake winked and flashed back at Sellett and his clients, the rolling landscape of the central Texas hill country stretching far beyond.

One of his visitors earlier in the day had remarked on the weather change, an early but temporary cool spell that confused the oaks and other deciduous trees, coaxing out the vivid autumn hues rarely seen this time of year. For this week at least, the landscape was closer to North Carolina or Virginia than Texas.

Unfortunately, Sellett had missed the views earlier in the day, enraptured in a conference call and the stacks of paper piled high across the burled walnut topping his desk. Only now, with the office long since closed and the sun below the horizon, did he regret missing the day's vistas outside his floor-to-ceiling windows. He let out a deep sigh after another swallow of scotch, cursing himself for failing to appreciate the things that brought him to Austin in the first place. Like most residents of these parts, Sellett fought through the hundred-degree summers by anticipating days like this, when people here knew for sure that they had chosen the best place in the world to live.

Sellett ingested another mouthful of single malt as he looked at his glory wall, where he displayed the diplomas, certificates, and pictures that made his clients feel good about the hefty fees paid to Rayburn Williams & Dodd, a Washington firm founded in 1902. Rayburn Williams had offices in five cities, contacts all over the world, clients in every industry imaginable, three hundred thirty-six lawyers, and a well-earned reputation for taking no prisoners. Nineteen years after joining the firm, Sellett had done absolutely nothing but enhance that reputation.

Sellett held the distinction of being the first lawyer in the history of the firm to become a partner in fewer than eight years. He'd been determined to make partner in seven years, just to beat the firm record. He made it in five. The day had been captured in a photograph of Sellett and the managing partner of the firm, which now constituted a portion of the shrine on the shelves of the antique hutch in the corner of Sellett's office.

"You need a picture of a wife and some kids on that shelf."

Sellett turned to see his partner Paul Jackson leaned against the doorframe. "That might be nice," he said. "Somebody waiting at home to have dinner, maybe go to a Little League game."

"Maybe a dog, too," Jackson said. "A yellow lab would suit you well."

Sellett took another sip. "Hell, I'd miss the Little League game and be late for dinner anyway. The dog would be cool, though. Want a belt before you leave?"

"Who said anything about leaving?" Jackson raised a handful of folders. "I had to get a couple of files from my paralegal's office and saw your light on."

"How do you work these hours with a family?"

"Nobody in my family knows me," Jackson said. "Probably best that way. I'm a miserable son of a bitch to live with."

"We love you, pal," Sellett said as he raised his glass.

Jackson looked over Sellett's shoulder at the shelves of framed photographs, one of which showed a shiny Cobalt ski boat, a smiling Sellett at the helm. "Is that your new boat?"

"Yeah, out on Lake Travis last month." Sellett shook his head. "I haven't been on it much."

"It's a twenty-footer, isn't it?

"Twenty-three including the ski platform," Sellett said with pride.

"I thought you'd be on it the whole summer," Jackson said.

"Me, too." Sellett sighed. "That's the reason I moved to Austin in the first place. Maybe I'll get a chance to get out more this fall."

"You should grab a client and get out this weekend," Jackson said. "A UT football game, a boat ride, a little golf. It could be fun."

"Great idea. Why don't you come along, Paul?"

Jackson shook his head. "No can do. Two soccer games on Saturday, and the in-laws are coming in town for the festivities. I'm thinking about working on a trial brief this weekend just to get away."

"If you change your mind, I'll probably line up something with Senator Dunbar," Sellett said. "He'll be busy with several things of interest to our clients in the legislature."

"Work hard on that for us, Bill. We'll need all the votes we can get to finish the job on tort reform."

"We need to be careful," Sellett said. "We get the tort reform they want and our clients won't need us anymore."

"Perfect," Jackson said with a smile. "We'll go to work for the other side. We'll reform the reforms, and start all over again. I have three kids who want to go to college."

Sellett chuckled and raised his glass, but wondered whether Jackson was serious. As much as he enjoyed the jousting, Sellett couldn't imagine the raw avarice required to endlessly stir the pot. Or could he? "That's a job for the trial lawyers," he said.

"Are you joking?" Jackson said. "Those guys aren't in your league."

"They're talented lawyers," Sellett argued. "They're smart and committed. Their problem is that they're basically competitors with each other."

"They can't spend their way to victory, Bill," Jackson countered. "Only our side has the money to do that."

"Is that how we did it last time?" Sellett asked. "Did we buy tort reform?"

"Of course not," Jackson said with a grin. "Tort reform passed because people who file lawsuits are evil, and their lawyers are worse. It passed because we needed it to put an end to our state's long and troubled history of frivolous lawsuits against doctors and hospitals." Jackson raised his fist in a righteous salute. "We needed tort reform so Texas could take its rightful place of glory and leadership in this great nation."

Sellett applauded. "I'm waiting for the band to play *Texas, Our Texas*. Great speech."

"Thanks. You should work on yours."

"I should work on my what?" Sellett asked.

"Think big, Bill," Jackson said. "You're forty-five. It's time to make some plans. With your background, your connections, and your looks, you should think big."

"I'm not following you, Paul."

"Here's what I'm thinking. You meet a woman in her early thirties, have a couple of sons, then get yourself elected Governor. After your first term, it'll be on to Congress or the Senate. Just remember me when you get there."

Sellett let out a hearty laugh. "The job's finally gotten to you, pal. Time to go home."

Jackson pointed a finger at Sellett as he left. "Don't forget it was my idea."

Sellett looked out at the twinkling lights of the city, stretching to the south and west. As he sat alone, he thought about his conversation with Jackson. Maybe he was right. Maybe it was time to adjust his sights. Draining the last of the cool, smoky scotch, Sellett allowed himself a contented smile. The possibilities were endless.

# CHAPTER 7

About ten miles out of Fort Worth, Grant felt the pressure slip away. Although he loved living in Fort Worth, the strain of his job paid no attention to the clock. At the end of each day, when he wanted to set down his work and focus on family, friends, and himself, he found himself instead worrying about cases, deadlines, and the phone calls he'd been unable to return. One of his law professors once said the law was like a jealous mistress. To Grant, it seemed more like a prison guard, complete with handcuffs, a billy club, and a nasty disposition.

He'd found a few ways to alleviate the stress while still in town, but by far the best way he knew was to head to the Hill Country, west and south of Fort Worth. Many people neither understood nor shared his affinity for this part of the state, preferring instead the piney woods of east Texas. But to Grant, the sparse, rugged terrain was simply beautiful. He was especially fond of Possum Kingdom Lake and his lake cottage. There, he could retreat to his thoughts if he needed to be alone, to the countryside if he wanted to hunt quail or turkey, or gather with friends and family for badly needed recharging of the batteries. It was only about an hour from home, but it was truly worlds away.

Grant and Leslie had an appointment in San Antonio to meet with Dr. Perkins. Although he was familiar with him from depositions, Grant needed to establish a rapport and talk at length about the Haller case. He was also anxious to see the laser surgery facility in San Antonio, one of only three in the world. The drive would allow Grant time to discuss the case with Leslie.

Grant drove from Fort Worth to San Antonio by a different route than most. Interstate thirty-five went directly from Fort Worth to Austin to San Antonio, about 190 miles. A calculator and a map would tell you that you could make the trip at the posted speed limit in about four hours, allowing for stops and a certain amount of traffic.

Grant despised the feeling of being boxed in between eighteen wheelers at seventy miles an hour, so he took Highway 281 instead. In contrast to the three or four lanes of traffic on each side of the divided highway found on the interstate, this road was just that. Sometimes four lanes, sometimes two. Sometimes divided by a median, sometimes not. Grant drove through Cleburne and picked up 281 in Hico, where he headed south through such scenic burgs as Hamilton, Lampasas, Burnet, Marble Falls, and Johnson City before heading into San Antonio.

In Burnet, they stopped for a Blizzard at Dairy Queen. Grant considered the Blizzard nothing short of genius and a sure sign, to paraphrase Ben Franklin, that God loves us and wants us to be happy. Vanilla soft serve ice cream blended with ingredients to form part sundae and part milkshake.

On the Blizzard menu one could find the tropical, with strawberries, bananas, and coconut, or the Georgia Mud Fudge, with brownies and chocolate sauce. Grant, however, always ordered what he referred to as the Mercer Blizzard, with chopped pecans, caramel sauce, and hot fudge. It was like eating a gooey, perfectly baked brownie with ice cream on top. Leslie passed. She was the only woman Grant knew who didn't like dessert.

As he drove, he ate the Blizzard slowly, running the spoon along the inside of the cup to scoop up the melting concoction at the perfect consistency. This made it difficult to sing along to the music blaring from the sound system of Grant's black Chevy Tahoe, for which Leslie was ever grateful. As he enjoyed his Blizzard and tapped his foot to the tunes of Bono and Don Henley, he ran through the Haller case with Leslie, focusing on details and trying to cement their understanding of the medical issues.

"Seven-year-old girl, complaining of headaches, with increasing frequency, intensity, and duration," Grant said. "No satisfactory response to medication. No link to activity or diet. After three months with no improvement, her pediatrician sent her to a neurologist for evaluation. Her neurologist conducted a brief office exam and prescribed a muscle relaxant, based on his belief that the little girl was under stress."

"Seven-year-olds have stress?" Leslie arched an eyebrow.

"Her mother said the same thing," Grant said as he spooned more of the Blizzard into his mouth. "She told the neurologist he was nuts. Then she realized she knew several people who'd become nearly inconsolable when their children had been denied admission to the best private *kindergarten* in town."

"This is one of your jokes, right?" Leslie shook her head.

"I'm serious, Leslie. Wait until you have children. Parents emphasize how important it is that their kids get into the best private elementary school, high school, college, and graduate school. These kids have all manner of stress-related illnesses. Chronic diarrhea, asthma attacks, the works. Probably the crushing sense of failure."

Leslie thumbed through the medical record summary in her lap. "What's wrong with these people? Can't they just let their kids play in the dirt?"

"I don't know," Grant said. "Anyway, Julie Haller stayed quiet, and when the frequency and severity of the headaches seemed to diminish for several weeks, she chalked it up as one of those things that just happens." Grant shoveled another spoonful of Blizzard into his mouth.

"The headaches came back. Mildly at first, then with a vengeance. Julie took Jennifer back to the neurologist, Dr. Purser, who told her stress was probably the culprit. Allergies were hitting everyone particularly hard that year, he said, especially children. When she asked about taking x-rays or CT scans, Dr. Purser shook his head and told her, surely in his most comforting and reassuring tone, that Jennifer would be fine. Said to bring her back in six months if she's still having problems."

"There's nothing in the notes about a request for a CT scan," Leslie said.

"I know," Grant said. "Julie insists they talked about it. Anyhow, four months later, Jennifer had the same symptoms. Purser told Julie there was nothing to worry about. This time, that wasn't good enough."

"I would hope not." Leslie flipped the page. "Did she get a referral to a different doctor?"

"I guess she figured her pediatrician would defend Purser, so she called a friend whose husband had seen a doctor for migraines. After a few phone calls, she and Jennifer wound up seeing Scott Raines, a pediatric neurologist. Raines examined Jennifer and heard what she'd gone through for the past year. According to Julie, Dr. Raines heard enough after about five minutes and ordered a CT scan. He said it had to be done the same day."

Leslie had the summary open to the page covering the CT scan, which had revealed a tumor in Jennifer's brain, located near the center of her head. The tumor was exerting pressure on the brain, which caused the headaches, as well as the nausea and vomiting. "I love radiology reports," she said. "They're so clinical. 'Multiple axillary views demonstrate increased signal density at level forty-six in the central cerebellar region. Suspicion is high for malignancy, which should be clinically correlated and perhaps confirmed by biopsy.' In English, that means, 'This little girl probably has cancer, and if she's throwing up all the time and complaining of headaches, you should probably cut her head open and see if this is as bad as I think it is.' Why can't they just say it like that?"

Grant cut a glance at her from the corner of his eye. "Would you?"

When the results came back to Dr. Raines, he conveyed them to Julie in person. He sat next to her in front of his desk as he described the unthinkable in plain terms, holding her hand and pausing now and then to let her dab at her eyes with a small embroidered handkerchief.

Julie quizzed Raines extensively about details and treatment options. He told her the tumor was located in the worst possible place, the center of the brain, where surgery couldn't be done without extensive damage to healthy tissue. In all likelihood, conventional surgery would leave Jennifer vegetative, if not dead. Julie asked about other facilities in the country that might have better doctors or more experience with this condition. Again, Raines explained that the medical literature on the subject came from hospitals and doctors around the country, indeed around the world. He was quite sure conventional surgery wasn't the answer.

"What about radiation?" Julie asked.

"At one time, radiation would have been perfect," Raines reported sadly, "but that time has passed."

Julie was stunned. "What are you talking about?"

"This particular type of cancer is well documented," Raines explained. "We think it's an astrocytoma, either the anaplastic variety or the pylocytic kind. A biopsy could tell us for sure, but we'll talk about that later. It's located in the cerebellum, near the brain stem, so it's difficult to reach surgically and extremely risky.

"The tumor is a little less than five centimeters in diameter, about the size and shape of a cherry. These tumors almost always double in size every four to six months. So, six months ago, when Jennifer's complaints were fairly new, we can say with pretty good certainty it was right around two centimeters. That's the cutoff size. If we radiate a two-centimeter mass in the brain, the chances of survival for a patient Jennifer's age is about ninety percent. Once it gets to five centimeters, radiation doesn't work."

Julie Haller's shoulders sagged. "What are her odds now?"

"Not good, I'm afraid," said Raines. "About a third of patients at this stage survive more than a year. But cancer treatment is individual. You can't go by statistics."

Julie looked straight at him, piercing his eyes with hers. "Don't patronize me, doctor. How long does she have?"

"Without surgery, I'd say four months. Six at the outside," Raines said.

"You just said surgery was impossible," Julie said.

"We can't do conventional surgery. There's an experimental treatment that might help. It's dangerous, and still in the testing phase, but it might be worth looking into. As I said, the location of the tumor means surgery could result in blindness, paralysis, loss of motor skills, or even death."

Julie's eyes prompted Raines to continue.

"It's laser surgery," he said. "Some doctors at Vanderbilt started looking into it a few years ago. They use what's called a free electron laser, which can be fine-tuned.

"Usually, a laser works in surgery by rapidly heating the water contained within the cells, causing a miniature explosion. This does less harm to the surrounding tissue than a metal scalpel, but the heat from the explosions still does some damage. The free electron laser is tuned to heat the water in the cells at a different wavelength, which results in a gentler explosion.

"A neurosurgeon at the UT medical school in San Antonio has worked on the technique. He's modified the laser for surgery on the brain. I've seen some of the literature, and it looks promising. There's a down side; one patient actually died on the table, and a couple of the patients early in the trials suffered injury to speech and motor centers of the brain. In those cases, the surgery was a success, but the complications to the patient were catastrophic.

"After those experiences, the surgeon continued his modifications and fine-tuning of the laser. Nothing so severe has happened since then, but there have been other instances where the patient was injured."

"If I understand this correctly," Julie said, "my daughter will die unless this surgery is performed on her. The risk is that she'll live, but may have some brain damage. Am I with you so far?"

"You are."

"Do I also understand that this surgery is most often successful, and that the majority of the patients aren't significantly injured by the procedure?"

"Yes, ma'am. That seems to be the case."

"Then I don't understand the problem."

"Because it's experimental, most insurance plans don't pay for it," said Raines.

"I doubt that will be a problem," Julie countered, her expression brightening for the first time since they started their discussion. "My husband is in the military, and we have Castle Guard as part of his insurance plan. I feel sure they'll pay for the surgery."

"That sounds promising." Raines nodded. "But I've heard that before. The program with the laser surgery is run and funded by the university, but the manufacturer of the laser charges a license fee of $150,000 every time it's used in surgery. The doctors might waive their fee if the university approves, but the hospital won't do it for free just on a whim, and the application and review process will take too long to help your daughter. The red tape involved in getting any other kind of funding will make it impossible for Jennifer to have surgery in time."

"So Castle Guard Insurance is our last hope?" Julie wondered aloud. She thanked Dr. Raines and left the office quickly. Her stomach churned at the prospect of her daughter's life depending on the decision of an insurance company.

GREG McCARTHY

# CHAPTER 8

Julie Haller was cautiously optimistic when she left Dr. Raines's office, but that feeling would give way to despair over the next couple of weeks. The first hint came when she talked to the people in the business office of the San Antonio laser surgery center, who let her know that the laser manufacturer never waived the license fee, and no insurance company had yet approved payment for the surgery. Incredulous, Julie reminded them that her husband was a Marine officer currently deployed in Iraq, and that they had the best medical insurance plan available. The woman in the insurance department told Julie they hadn't seen any military families in the short time the program had been in existence.

"You never know," she said, "but it sure seems like the military would make sure their people and their families get the treatment they need."

"How much time will it take to check?" asked Julie.

"Usually a couple of days, but I can ask them to expedite the process, considering your daughter's condition."

The news actually took far less time to arrive. By the time Julie had returned from running a couple of errands, she had a message from San Antonio. Castle Guard declined to pay for the procedure, because it was experimental and used equipment not approved for the surgery to be performed.

Nerves jangling, Julie got on the phone with Castle Guard. First, she encountered the computer phone tree, which answered the call in the same female robotic voice used around the country and led her through the dizzying maze of "for benefits, press two" and "to add or change policyholder information, press seven." When the first nine options failed to offer the chance to talk to someone about changing the decision to deny a surgical procedure that would save her daughter's life, she pressed "0" and was instructed to hold. Six times she was told that her call would be answered in the order in which it was received, and twice the female robot informed her that she could call back at a later time when call volume was likely to be less of a problem. Thirty-five minutes after placing the call, a real person greeted her and asked how she could help.

"For starters, you can pay for my daughter's medical care like you agreed to do in the first place."

"Please give me the claim number, ma'am."

Julie apologized, gave her the claim number, and offered the five-minute version of the story, up to the point of Castle Guard's denial of the procedure.

"It'll cost about $200,000," Julie explained. "My daughter has a brain tumor and this is the only way to fix it."

"I note from the file that the procedure is experimental," droned the newest member of the Castle Guard claim denial team, "and the policy doesn't cover experimental procedures."

"It's only experimental because the laser is not yet approved by the FDA for this particular surgery. They've already approved it for about a dozen other things, and the approval for this procedure is pending." Julie was sure this would resonate, and the person on the other end of the line would realize that the policy exclusion wasn't intended to be a death sentence for an eight-year-old girl.

"If it's not approved for this surgery, then this surgery is considered experimental," said the claim denial specialist, sounding more like the female robot in the telephone tree.

"Then I need to speak to your supervisor."

The jump in authority wasn't much help. The supervisor was the captain of the claim denial team at Castle Guard and had no interest in putting his neck on the line by committing the company to pay for unapproved laser surgery.

Julie quickly saw this was getting nowhere. She asked the supervisor to connect her to his boss or anyone else who had the authority to approve the payment. She was told no such person existed.

"How can that be?" she demanded. "Are you telling me there's nobody at your company who can make a decision?"

"What I'm telling you, miss, is that the policy clearly states we're not required to pay for experimental surgery. We're not saying your daughter can't have the surgery."

That sent Julie over the edge. "You heartless son of a bitch," she screamed. "Do you realize this operation costs $200,000? Do you personally have that kind of money to spare? I DON'T. My husband is fighting in Iraq. Castle Guard collects millions of dollars in premiums every month from military families. And now you say you won't pay for the surgery to save my daughter's life?"

The supervisor disconnected the call after "son of a bitch," and the rest of Julie's tirade had been delivered to herself. Not that she blamed him. Castle Guard probably didn't pay him enough to listen to her scream at him and call him names.

Julie's next call was to the Marine Family Liaison Office. After the first Gulf War, the military realized the families of their active duty personnel suffered greatly when spouses and parents were deployed overseas. Largely through the efforts of the first female Air Force Colonel to command a wing of the Strategic Air Command, the military initiated programs to help those families. Financial advice, help with contractors for home repair, and assistance with transportation for children to after-school events were all available. The program also included support with insurance, including medical care coverage.

The officer assigned to the Haller case was a young Lieutenant named Lance Fisher. He told Julie he wanted to help her; her argument made sense. Still, he said, he'd seen the policy language about experimental surgery, and figured it might be tough to get the approval they needed.

A couple days later, Julie got the call from Fisher with the bad news. He told her that the supervisor to whom she'd spoken was disciplined for hanging up on her, but the claims manager had denied payment as well, citing the same policy provisions.

"Is there anything we can do?" Julie pleaded.

"I've asked my commander to get involved," Fisher said. "He wants to meet you this afternoon."

Julie's spirits rose when she met Colonel Marcus Hanson. Though his eyes sparkled kindly when he greeted Julie, she could tell those eyes carried an edge honed in combat. She'd seen the same look in her husband's eyes when he had come back from his first tour of duty in Iraq.

"Marcus Hanson," he said in a mellifluous baritone while taking her hand in a strong but courteous handshake, "Please have a seat."

Julie figured Hanson's voice, along with his position in the Marine Corps, would be enough to make the Castle Guard pencil pushers shake in their cheap cubicles.

"Lt. Fisher has given me the highlights," said Hanson. "Why don't you fill in the gaps so we can try to get this thing done."

Julie started with the visit to Dr. Raines and walked Hanson through the medical diagnosis and treatment options for Jennifer's tumor, ending with her difficult journey through the Castle Guard claims department.

"We've been successful a few times in getting them to change their minds," Hanson told her, "but I have to tell you, the word on the street is that Castle Guard upper management has decided to stick to their guns on cases like this. Last year, they paid out about eighty million dollars in claims they originally denied. That money comes straight off the bottom line, and it's a number they don't want to see again. The executives at the company are nervous, including their new CEO, a fellow named Lewis Cashman.

"This guy is ruthless. The man he replaced was supposedly his best friend. Cashman set him up with the board of directors, whispering in their ears that the company could do better with new leadership. He even sabotaged two deals that would've saved the guy's job then resurrected those deals as soon as he took over. I heard there were a few questionable transactions, including the deal with the Defense Department for major medical insurance."

"How can he get away with that sort of thing?" Julie asked.

"Castle Guard's stock dropped twelve percent the year before Cashman took over. If that happens again, Cashman and all of his people will be out on the street. He looked around and figured that denying benefits is the easiest place to make up the eighty million. The stock has rebounded nicely."

"You make it sound hopeless." Julie's shoulders sagged.

"Maybe not," said Hanson. "The military and its families spend about ten billion a year with Castle Guard on premiums. The program comes up for renewal every year, and sooner or later competition kicks in. There are plenty of insurance companies out there who would love to have the ten billion in premium."

"So what do we do?"

"I've already put in a call to the vice president at Castle Guard in charge of our account," Hanson said. "I expect to talk to him today or tomorrow. He might be our best shot at getting this thing on the right track."

"Is there anything else I can do?" Julie asked.

"Just take care of Jennifer and wait for my call."

Julie Haller left Hanson's office thinking her luck had turned. But the call from Hanson wasn't good, and it came after another call with the news about her husband's injuries. Julie often heard the old bromide that what doesn't kill you makes you stronger. All she knew now was that she felt dangerously close to the line.

# CHAPTER 9

As Grant and Leslie finished running through the details of the case, they drove into the northern outskirts of San Antonio. It amazed Grant how fast the place continued to grow.

"Every time I drive through here, San Antonio gets closer and closer to actually merging with Austin," he said absently.

"It wasn't like this when you grew up here?" Leslie asked.

"No way." He shook his head. "In those days, it was about thirty minutes from Austin to San Marcos, and another thirty to San Antonio. Now it's a continuous chain of Chili's restaurants, Courtyard by Marriott hotels, and discount outlet malls."

"My hometown doesn't even have a Hampton Inn yet." Leslie chuckled.

The medical center at the University of Texas at San Antonio, like most medical centers more than twenty years old, was an endless maze of corridors connecting old buildings with new expansion. Parking was a nightmare, and it took them twenty minutes to work their way through the labyrinth of hallways and find the office of Dr. Richard Perkins. Grant was shocked at what he found.

In the practice of law, particularly at large firms, square footage and finish in a lawyer's office is highly prized. Partners often work in offices exceeding three or four hundred square feet. Even new associates typically have their own private offices with windows. Space and furnishings are signs of power, success and respect.

The medical field often has no such pretension. Medical school is, in large part, a clinical experience more than a classroom experience. Before being set free to treat patients on their own, doctors get two to four years of intense, hands-on training with older and more experienced physicians watching their every move. The need for a spacious, lavish office isn't even considered.

Despite his awareness of all this, Grant recoiled in horror when he peered into Perkins' office and saw nothing short of utter chaos. Papers, both single and in stacks by the hundred, formed a pile on Perkins's desk that Grant figured at about two feet high. Unused inboxes and outboxes provided rudimentary bookends. Cheap ball point pens lay scattered everywhere, and medical textbooks, open to a chapter of interest to Dr. Perkins at some time or another, served as paperweights. Grant wondered whether the entire pile would fall or simply blow away if one of the textbooks was removed.

Behind the pile sat Dr. Perkins. Each time they'd previously met, Grant had been impressed. This time was no exception. Perkins was barely short of six feet, with a swimmer's lanky build. Flowing jet black hair set off the angular features of his face and complemented the goatee and the olive skin of his Mediterranean descent. Fashionable black eyeglasses with a silver bar across the top of each lens gave him an erudite air and perfectly complemented the tailored Armani suit, custom shirt, and Italian silk tie. The contrast between Perkins and his office was alarming, but a quick glance at Leslie let Grant know that she hadn't noticed the clutter.

Perkins stood. "Hello, Mr. Mercer. Nice to see you again."

"This is my legal assistant, Leslie Roberts. I appreciate you meeting with us."

"A pleasure," Perkins said with a bow toward Leslie. "Please call me Rick. I remember Jennifer Haller and her mom, and it was the least I could do to make some time for you today."

That, and the six grand I sent, thought Grant.

"By the way, I talked to my assistant already, and she'll have a refund check for you when you leave here today," said Perkins.

"Really?" asked Grant, wondering whether he'd thought aloud. "I must say I understood from the beginning you would charge your usual fee, and that's okay with me."

"Sorry about that," said Perkins. "When you called, you mentioned the procedure and the possibility of working as an expert on the plaintiff's side. Usually that means my highest fee, but I'd just come out of about seven hours of surgery, and if you mentioned Jennifer by name, I missed it."

"Are you telling me you're not going to help?" Grant felt his anger simmer. "The least you could have done was extend a little professional courtesy by calling and saving me the drive from Fort Worth."

"You misunderstand, Mr. Mercer."

"Call me Grant."

"All right, Grant. You misunderstand," said Perkins with a smile. "I'd be happy to help you with your case, but I won't accept a fee."

Grant was stunned. "You're right, Rick. I don't understand."

"You know about our program from the depositions you've taken," Perkins began, "but I think this is the first time our paths have crossed involving the new laser surgery. This is truly revolutionary. And it works. We've successfully operated on thirty-two patients in the first eighteen months. We've had three patients suffer complications, and our critics point to that complication rate to justify the lack of approval of the laser for this procedure.

"We're developing a new laser specifically for use in brain surgery, but the prototype is at least a year away. Approval and manufacture on the scale needed will add about three years, and another three will go by while we train surgeons to use it. So, six to eight years from now, this 'experimental' surgery will be almost commonplace, but in the meantime several hundred patients like Jennifer Haller will die when we could have prevented it."

"I like a crusade as much as the next guy," replied Grant, "but why do this for free? You charged fees in all of the cases you did for the doctors."

"Sure I did. That money came from their insurance companies," Perkins said. "Can you think of a good reason not to take money from an insurance company?"

When Grant's wry smile was the only reply, he continued. "If I have it right, your clients will ultimately pay for my fees, and for the other costs you incur in this case."

"That's right," Grant said, "unless we lose, in which case I have to eat them."

"Well, we're all big boys here, aren't we?" Perkins said with a gleam in his eye. "No offense, Leslie."

"None taken." Leslie blushed.

"Still, it wouldn't be right for me to get paid only if you lose the case, would it? No, you can count me in, Grant. No charge."

Perkins rose, leaning against the bookshelf behind his desk. He picked up a carved wooden rhinoceros, carefully inspecting the tusk of highly polished teak as he spoke.

"Julie Haller came to see me, with Jennifer. She said she was having trouble with their insurance company. I told her I'd waive my fee and talk to the hospital about waiving the charges there. We were down to about one-fifty for the surgery, but we can't get the laser company to comp the license fee. They have shareholders to answer to, and it just doesn't work out. Then Castle Guard does their usual, and Jennifer suffers the consequences.

"Much as I'd like to criticize the insurance company for not approving the surgery, it's probably not my place in this lawsuit. The important thing is that Jennifer Haller could have survived. She shouldn't have even needed my help."

"Give me the short explanation of that, if you will." Grant was intrigued. He saw Leslie scribbling furiously on a yellow pad.

"Jennifer's tumor was one we see quite often," Perkins said. "It seeds in the brainstem or cerebellum and grows slowly. It takes two to three years to get to two centimeters and tends to stay there a year to eighteen months. The good news for most patients is that they start to experience symptoms during that time. If we can catch it before it starts to grow again, we can probably remove it without damaging the adjacent areas of the brain." Perkins returned to the cheap chair at his disheveled desk, rubbing his temples and letting out a long sigh.

"If it's not detected during that window, the chances of successful surgery go down dramatically. These things tend to be in a part of the brain right next door to the centers controlling speech, motor skills, and higher cognitive function. When it grows into one or more of those areas, surgery just does too much damage to remove it safely. Most of those patients died on the table, and most of the survivors came out permanently damaged."

Perkins rummaged around on his desk for a moment before reaching into the middle of the pile, pulling out a large manila folder

THE PRICE OF LIFE

marked "X-rays." Grant looked on in amazement at Perkins' ability to find the needle in the haystack of paper inhabiting the desktop.

"I looked at the CT scans they took a few months before she died," Perkins continued. "I can tell you just about for sure the tumor was two centimeters or less when she first started complaining about her headaches."

"Let's start there," Grant interrupted. "If I were on the other side, I'd wonder how you could possibly make that statement when you didn't have a CT when her headaches began."

"We don't need one," Perkins explained. "The medical literature is clear. Considering the typical growth rate of these tumors, estimating the size of the tumor a year before a CT is simple math. There are thousands of cases in the literature, and the statistical error rate is less than three percent. I feel sure you already went through this with Dr. Howard."

"Did you tell him we're working with Dr. Howard?" Grant asked Leslie, visibly startled.

Leslie shook her head.

"Fred and I have known each other for years," Perkins said. "He called me last week to talk about you. He said to tell you hello, Leslie. Dr. Howard reminded me about Jennifer Haller. How is her dad, by the way?"

"He's one tough son of a gun," said Grant. "He comes to San Antonio a couple of times a week, to the prosthesis center run by the Fallen Heroes Fund."

"I wouldn't wish that man's year on my worst enemy, or even a plaintiffs' lawyer," Perkins said.

Grant couldn't tell right away whether Perkins was serious. "Back to Jennifer's case," he said, "Even if they had found the tumor with a CT scan, and it was the size you say, how do we know the surgery would have been successful and without complications?"

"We can't be absolutely certain," answered Perkins. "But if you ask me whether I have an opinion about that, based on reasonable medical probability, I'll tell you I think there's about a ninety-five percent chance Jennifer Haller would be alive and healthy today if they'd just taken the damn CT scan."

# CHAPTER 10

For weeks after they met with Grant Mercer, Julie Haller refused to actively participate in the case. The shock of her daughter's death, coupled with the need to assist in her husband's grueling rehabilitation, had taken a terrible toll. Julie slept little, ate less, and slowly withdrew from her usual routines. Adding a lawsuit to her plate just didn't sound appealing.

Julie Haller, however, was not one to sit still for long. She had eventually come to grips with her husband's new physical challenges and with the need for him to handle more of the load himself. She had to care for her son, even if every day without her daughter was an emotional black hole. Over time, she began to deal with the loss of her child by delving deeply into the issues surrounding their case.

After dinner one night, Julie sat with Ed on their back porch, a warm summer breeze wafting softly across them, rustling her blonde tresses and providing a comforting caress to begin the evening after a muggy afternoon.

"I'm telling you, Ed, the more I dig the angrier I get," Julie said.

"Then why keep digging? We have a lawyer. Let him handle it."

"That's part of the problem. Remember that new law Mr. Mercer told us about? Well, here's the deal. Insurance companies and doctors had been pushing to get that kind of law passed for years. They started putting caps on things in the seventies, then put in requirements for reports, then got this bill passed by promising everyone insurance rates would go down."

"Okay," said Haller. "That's what happened, right?"

"Not really. One company froze its rates. The doctors themselves own that company. Nobody else lowered their rates. In fact, they all charge more now than they did before."

"How do they pull that off?" asked Haller. "I thought the insurance department controlled that kind of stuff."

"That's what they're supposed to do. Trouble is, everybody down there is in everyone else's pocket. Remember when I used to work for Prime?"

"Yeah."

"We used to try to get help from the insurance department when we got gouged on rates. They were useless. They're still no help. Only a few complaints have even been filed with the department, and there hasn't been so much as a public hearing. All complaints have been dismissed with no explanation. And all the rate increases have been approved."

"Where are you finding all this stuff?"

"Most of it's on the Internet. The state government has its own site, with all the departments linked. You can find out about registered lobbyists, campaign finances for the legislators, and the way the committees are structured. It's not hard."

Haller let out a deep sigh. "Does it surprise you that insurance rates haven't changed?"

"Not at all," Julie responded. "But when I looked closer I found out all these people have connections. For instance, there's a state senator whose company is in the insurance business. His company is represented by a lawyer who's also a lobbyist in Austin, and that lobbyist was a main player in the passage of the statute."

"Sounds normal to me." Haller shrugged.

"What if I told you the senator was the head of the committee that wrote the bill?"

"Still sounds normal. That's how the government works."

"Well, it shouldn't be," Julie said, her voice catching in her throat. "Our daughter is dead because of Dr. Purser, and they put a lid on how much we can get if we win our case. No attorney's fees, no interest, nothing else. They defined our loss, Ed. They put a price tag on Jennifer."

As she spoke, the anger turned to raw pain, and tears soon flowed down Julie's smooth cheeks. Her breath came in short, sniffled spasms, and she squeezed her eyes tightly shut, hoping to erase reality and find a way to mend her shattered heart.

Haller did his best to keep his wife from the edge of collapse. He'd learned by now to hold her tightly, stay quiet, and let the worst of the pain subside. He brought her head closer to his shoulder, hoping she could feel the comfort of his arm around her. He softly kissed the top of her head as the tears slowed and her breathing returned to normal.

"It's not fair, Ed. It's just not fair."

Feeling his wife's agony stirred his anger, and it rose quickly. His gut tightened and his heart raced as the rage built, but his face betrayed nothing.

# CHAPTER 11

State Senator Ken Dunbar wore a relaxed smile as he walked out the front door of his Possum Kingdom lake house and headed to his Cadillac Escalade. Dunbar loved his time at the lake, more now than ever with his log cabin-style mansion. The home sat perched on a cliff ninety-five feet above the water, with a spectacular sunset view from the wrap-around porch. An elevator carried his family and guests to the floating dock, which housed his ski boat, fishing boat, party barge, and a small flotilla of personal water craft. The dock itself was far too large to pass inspection if currently built, but was grandfathered in as a remodel.

Now serving his fourth term as a state senator from Temple, Dunbar was a senior member of the Joint Committee on Civil Justice and chairman of the Senate Natural Resources Committee. He was the highest-ranking elected official with direct control over the state's 235 man-made lakes, plus the only natural lake in Texas. With that position came more power than most people realized, especially when dealing with governmental agencies like the Brazos River Authority.

The BRA controlled the chain of reservoirs created at various points of the Brazos River, including Possum Kingdom. The authority owned about fourteen thousand acres of real estate along the shoreline, estimated to be worth eighty million dollars. The BRA leased the dirt to individuals and families, who owned the houses, garages, and boat docks.

For more than fifty years, lake houses were bought and sold without much ado, leases were extended and renewed, and people passed their houses to succeeding generations. The new BRA board, however, saw the mission of the agency much differently, and hired a Houston consulting firm to help them turn the real estate into a profit center. The consultants correctly noted that Possum Kingdom had great commercial potential, and set about the task of recommending ways for the BRA to maximize the earnings potential of its holdings. New leases with higher rates were proposed, and a scheme devised to allow the Authority to claim homes as its own once leases expired.

The new plan, of course, met with much resistance. Dunbar's lake neighbors implored him to do what it took to put a stop to this insanity. Instead, Dunbar sold his original house just before the consultant's report was made public and bought a small, dilapidated cabin on one of the few lakefront lots not owned by the BRA. When he finished with the demolition of the old cabin and the construction of his dream home, he had a spectacular house with no BRA entanglements.

When a bill was presented requiring the Authority to sell the land at Possum Kingdom to its tenants, Dunbar used his position as chairman of the natural resources to kill it. This infuriated the sponsor of the bill, and Dunbar reluctantly relented. The other house of the legislature passed the bill on the final day of the session, giving the property owners at lake the opportunity to buy their land and removing the BRA from the property management business.

Naturally, this didn't set well with the BRA board. Lobbyists were phoned and the urgency of the situation explained. Those lobbyists in turn talked to Senator Dunbar, explaining how pleased they'd be if anything could be done on their behalf at this late juncture.

Dunbar had ascended to his position by knowing the rules of the game in the legislature. Just before midnight on the final night of the session, he officially recalled the bill to his committee, citing "transcription discrepancies." There were no such errors, of course, but with another two years before the legislature met again, the idea of the BRA selling property at Possum Kingdom would have to wait.

Senator Dunbar returned home after the session to find dozens of *For Sale* signs littering his front lawn. Next came nasty letters from constituents. Then, of course, the death threats started. As a result, he'd spent more time at his lake mansion in the months since the end of the session.

Dunbar eased the oversized SUV down the path and through the wrought iron gates keeping his home secluded from the road, noting with pleasure the calligraphic *D* on each gate, gold leaf in shining contrast to the black powder finish on the iron. He turned left and drove to the Trading Post in search of steaks for the evening's dinner, preoccupied with thoughts of boating and barbecue.

After gathering his rib eyes, corn on the cob, and salad items for dinner, Dunbar backed out of the store's parking lot and returned to the road. He immediately felt the Cadillac pulling to the left, the big SUV bucking and shaking as if driving on ancient cobblestones. He figured he could make it to the house and check it there, but about two miles down the road the ride got too rough, and Dunbar knew he would damage his $700 custom chrome rim if he kept driving on the flat tire.

"Son of a bitch." Dunbar sighed as he saw the tire, sidewall bulging over the tread like a fat man's belly over the waistband of his undersized pants. "Just what I need."

As he moved around the back of the SUV, an old gray pickup pulled up behind him and the driver swung the door open. "Need a hand?"

Dunbar knew very well how to change a tire, and was certainly capable of doing the job himself. As a state senator, however, he'd grown accustomed to having such menial tasks performed by others. Besides, from the looks of the pickup, the driver could use the twenty bucks Dunbar would offer for the favor. "Sure," he answered. "If you don't mind, I'd be obliged."

The stranger got out of the pickup and walked to the back of the Escalade, wearing a ball cap pulled down low over the ears and aviator glasses with oversized chrome frames. A neatly cropped beard, flecked with gray at the chin and cheeks, covered the lower half of the driver's face. The senator introduced himself, emphasizing the "senator" part.

"Got a jack?" the driver asked.

"Yeah, right," stammered Dunbar, subconsciously reaching for his wallet. "Let's get in there and get that stuff."

He raised the tailgate and leaned in, lifting the carpeted mat covering the rear cargo compartment of the Cadillac.

"Let me get that," said the voice behind him.

Dunbar straightened up, backing away from the bumper, and was confused in the next instant. He didn't exactly feel the blade slide across his throat. It was more like a sudden realization that something terrible had just happened, and he was powerless to do anything about it. Dunbar fell face-first into the back end of the SUV, blood foaming at the corners of his mouth and rushing from the gaping wound in his throat.

Casually wiping the five-inch steel blade on the leg of the senator's pants, the killer stepped back and slid behind the wheel. An hour later, the old gray pickup truck was back in its owner's garage, engine ticking and creaking as it cooled.

# CHAPTER 12

When Dunbar hadn't returned after an hour, his wife became annoyed. He'd often go on detours when they were at the lake, and she usually didn't mind. Today was different. Their guests, a banker from Dallas and his wife, would arrive soon, and she seldom liked to entertain her husband's business associates without him present. This was especially true with this particular couple, since the man was in his late fifties and his new wife had just turned twenty-eight. She could understand the desire some men had for younger companionship, but this guy's daughter from his first marriage was a year younger than her new stepmother. Getting younger at that position was one thing, but skipping an entire generation was another.

She dialed her husband's cell and for the third straight time got his voice mail. She knew Dunbar regarded his phone not as a luxury, but as an absolute necessity. While that was partly true, it didn't make her feel any better that his cell phone was, for the most part, more important to her husband than she was.

At the two-hour mark, with her guests present and her frustration mounting, she called the Trading Post. The cashier confirmed the senator had indeed been in that afternoon to buy steaks and groceries, but it had been at least an hour ago and she hadn't seen him since.

A couple of quick calls to friends around the lake brought no new information. He hadn't gone to see a friend and talk over a margarita or Bloody Mary. He hadn't gone to the marina to look at a wakeboard boat, and he hadn't stopped at the Rockin' S Saloon to get a cold beer and the latest gossip from the bartender. Mrs. Dunbar decided to take a look for herself.

As she walked out the front door and headed to her Mercedes sedan, she saw the BRA Ranger's Explorer enter the driveway, its blue and red lights flashing, and stopped cold. She'd never been the worrying kind and didn't usually assume the worst, but somehow she knew bad news was on its way the moment the Ranger stepped out from behind the wheel.

"Mrs. Dunbar, can we talk, ma'am? Inside the house might be best. It's about your husband."

The wife of State Senator Ken Dunbar felt her knees go weak, and the Ranger was barely able to slow her fall.

When she came to ten minutes later, she was lying on the sofa with the Ranger and her two house guests looking down at her.

"Mrs. Dunbar, are you okay?" the Ranger asked.

"I think so," she responded. "What happened?"

"You fainted."

"I know that, dammit," she said, her voice rising. "I mean, what are you doing here? You said something about my husband. Is he okay?"

As the Ranger broke the news, the young wife of the banker started to cry, looking as if she would become physically ill. The Ranger spared everyone present a detailed description of the scene, informing the senator's wife instead that they suspected criminal activity. Mercifully, he didn't describe it as "foul play." He told her the

Palo Pinto County Sheriff would be along shortly to ask her some questions and would probably need her to identify the body.

"Of course," she said numbly. She'd never imagined how she might react to the news of the murder of her husband, but this kind of detached emptiness would certainly not have been her guess. "When will he be here?"

# CHAPTER 13

Sheriff Ronnie Clyde Barlow fidgeted all the way to the Dunbar lake house. This was by far his least favorite part of the job. Usually, his biggest challenges were traffic control for parades on the Fourth of July and the occasional automobile accident on a remote county road. Lately, there had been more meth lab busts and other drug-related work, but violence was uncommon in Barlow's county. In his career as sheriff, he'd handled only about a dozen homicides, and their rarity was one reason he liked being the sheriff of a sparsely populated county.

As he wrapped up his questioning of Mrs. Dunbar, his thoughts shifted inevitably from the professional angle of the case to the personal side. He knew the senator, though not well, and occasionally had the chance to visit with his wife. The woman sitting across from Barlow at this moment bore little resemblance to what he remembered. This woman was practically catatonic, her eyes lifeless and flat. She answered all questions in the same monotone, and most people would have suspected a drug problem.

Barlow knew from experience that family members often had this reaction to such horrific news. For many, it was just too much to handle, and their minds simply shut down for awhile until they had a chance to recover.

"I think that's all for now," Barlow said. "We'll talk again tomorrow. My deputy will stay with you as long as you need, and we'll keep a close eye on your house. Are your children here with you?"

"No," she said weakly. "My daughter's coming, but she can't get here until tomorrow. I'll be fine for tonight."

Barlow nodded as he handed her a card. "If you change your mind, please just let me know."

The next day, Barlow accompanied Mrs. Dunbar as she identified the body of her husband and began making funeral arrangements. She was a bit disturbed at the thought of an autopsy, but Barlow assured her it was required due to the circumstances of the senator's death. She nodded slowly, unable to protest any further, and asked to be informed when the body could be released to the funeral home.

"Should be just a few days," said Barlow. "The autopsy will be done in Fort Worth, and you can let them know what arrangements you want to make from there."

"Thank you," she said before slowly walking away.

His questioning of Mrs. Dunbar was unproductive. She hadn't heard her husband speaking with anyone on the telephone before he left, and he hadn't mentioned any plans to meet with anyone on his way to or from the Trading Post. Yes, she knew her husband had a few enemies, but they were the political kind, more interested in ruining his reputation or his career than killing him.

She confirmed the death threats and said the Texas Rangers, whose responsibilities included security for state officials, had dismissed all of them, considering none to be credible. In short, she knew of nobody who would want to harm her husband and no reason anyone would want him dead.

Barlow inspected the Escalade, which was locked in the garage at his headquarters. A three-inch screw was embedded in left front tire at the junction of the sidewall and tread. This would account for a slow loss of air pressure, rather than a blowout. The SUV was equipped with the latest electronics, including tire pressure sensors. When the buttons on the dash were pressed in the proper sequence, a display showed eleven pounds of pressure per square inch on the left front tire.

The report from Barlow's deputy noted that the entire vehicle had been checked for fingerprints, and none were found. Searches for hair, fluids, fibers, and trace elements were likewise negative. The blood covering practically every square inch of the cargo area belonged to the senator, and none was from another source. No weapon was found at the scene or in the vehicle, although it was painfully obvious that the murder weapon had been a large, sharp knife.

Upon returning to his office, Barlow retrieved a message informing him that the Federal Bureau of Investigation would send its forensic team in the afternoon to assist in the investigation. The caller identified himself as Special Agent Kirk from the Fort Worth field office and reminded him that none of the evidence was to be disturbed.

Still wondering who would be assisting whom once the feds were involved, Barlow pored over the report for the fourth time that day, searching again for anything to help him solve the case. Hell, he was looking for anything that might tell him how to start to solve the case. No weapon. No evidence at the scene. No witness. No motive. Just a dead body in the back of a luxury SUV on a road in his county in the middle of a glorious Friday afternoon. And the body of a state senator, at that.

# CHAPTER 14

On a cloudless fall Saturday afternoon, Grant and Samantha Mercer drove fifteen miles to Weatherford for Bradley Haller's seventh birthday party. For decades, Weatherford had been a sleepy bedroom community to Fort Worth and the Parker County seat. Lately, natural gas exploration in the area had pumped millions into the local economy, and McMansions dotted the newer developments.

The Haller home was definitely not the result of the gas boom. The house was a rambler, modest but well-kept in an established neighborhood where forty-foot oak and pecan trees formed graceful canopies over quiet streets. Grant and Samantha turned the corner of the house and walked into the spacious back yard, him in jeans and a linen beach shirt and her wearing a simple sleeveless blouse with a black skirt stopping just above the knees.

"I'll introduce you to Ed and Julie first, then we can let them do the honors with the rest of the folks here," said Grant. "I honestly don't think we'll know anyone else."

Samantha nodded. She was shy, painfully so at times, but always willing to make the effort to meet the people in Grant's business circles. Once the initial contact was out of the way, she usually grew comfortable with other people rather quickly.

Grant led the way to the barbecue grill, where Ed Haller stood wearing an apron and wielding a spatula. "Ed, I'd like you to meet my wife, Samantha."

"Pleased to meet you, Samantha."

Samantha knew about the prosthesis, covered by Haller's khakis. She was less prepared for Haller's presence. He was tall and handsome, nearly the perfect physical specimen. Well over six feet and built like a gymnast, his square jaw and angular features went well with the standard Marine flattop. Samantha found the total package intimidating and reassuring at the same time. "Likewise, Ed."

"Let me get Julie over here," Haller said with a wave of his hand. Grant turned to see Julie Haller approaching in a patterned sun dress of gold and blue, the halter top revealing her tanned shoulders.

"Julie, you know Grant. This is his wife, Samantha."

"Thank you both for coming," said Julie. "I know it's a bit of a drive."

"No trouble at all," said Grant. "We're happy to be invited."

After a few minutes of small talk about hamburgers, cake, and ice cream, Julie took Samantha by the arm and left the men by the grill. She introduced Samantha to her parents, to Bradley, and to a couple of friends who'd stayed to watch over the kids. When Bradley announced that he wanted to join his friends in the bounce house, Julie let him in, then sat with Samantha on the gliding love seat beneath the red oak in the center of the yard.

"This is a nice party," Samantha offered to get the conversation going. "Your home is lovely."

"We've done a few fix-ups here and there," Julie said. We really like it here, with my parents close by. Schools are good, too."

"Bradley seems to be having a great time."

"He's a seven-year-old at his own birthday party." Julie laughed. "No better time, I suppose."

"Tell me a little about you, Julie. Where are you from? Where did you and Ed meet? What did you do before you had your kids?"

"I'm from around here. My folks moved to Weatherford when I was six. My dad worked for the city in the engineering department. My mom taught school.

"I started at North Texas and transferred after my first year to A&M. That's where I met Ed. He was a senior when I was a sophomore. He was in the corps of cadets and wore those high riding boots." Julie rolled her eyes at the memory.

"I know those boots." Samantha nodded. "All the way to the knee, polished like glass?"

"That's them," agreed Julie. "When I first saw them, I thought they were hideous. Then I saw Ed wearing them, and my opinion changed." An arched eyebrow told Samantha the reason for the change of heart.

"We dated off and on for awhile, and I tried to keep it from getting serious. Ed had committed to the Marines and was commissioned after graduation. We kept in touch for the next couple of years, while I finished my undergrad. We were married after I earned my Masters. Ed finished his Marine commitment at about the same time, and we moved to Fort Worth."

"If Ed finished with the Marines, how did he wind up in Iraq?" Samantha asked.

"That's how it is when you're in the reserves." Julie shrugged.

"Grant said he did four tours of duty."

"Yep." Julie nodded. "He was only supposed to go twice."

"What's that like, with him gone for months at a time?"

"I was a single parent while Ed was gone. I raised the kids, paid the bills, and worked at my own job."

"You had to go back to work?"

"Sure," Julie said. "Ed had a job with an engineering firm after leaving the Marines the first time, but he took a huge pay cut when they called him back. I used to work for a company called Prime Lending before Jennifer was born, but I'd already quit that job. I had to find a job with better hours so I could take care of Jen and Bradley. At least we're close to my parents. They were a big help. Ed's an only child, and his mom lives in San Antonio. His dad died right after Ed joined the Marines."

"Grant's from San Antonio, too," said Samantha, searching for something to keep the conversation on a more positive note.

"Ed actually grew up outside Kerrville, on a working ranch," said Julie. "Rode horses, fed cattle, all that stuff."

Samantha chuckled. "Grant might have ridden a pony at a petting zoo, but he's a city boy all the way."

"Nothing wrong with city boys. Where did you two meet?"

"In Lubbock, of all places," said Samantha. "He was finishing law school, and I was a senior in college. We met at a ten-K run."

"The athletic type, huh?"

"Absolutely," Samantha said with a grin. "He refuses to admit he's getting older."

"They all do that, don't they?" agreed Julie. "What about you? Do you still work?"

"Not these days," Samantha said. "I taught school for a few years, but we agreed I should stay home with our kids. Just about went back to work when Grant left the big firm."

Julie tilted her head. "Grant was with a big firm?"

"Yeah." Samantha nodded. "Five years in downtown Dallas."

"And he went from there to the firm he has now?"

"Oh, no. We moved to Fort Worth and Grant started a solo practice. He didn't even have a secretary for the first six months."

"That must have been an interesting time," Julie said. "What did you think?"

"I questioned his sanity, of course," said Samantha. "Life with the big firm was comfortable. Starting a solo practice wasn't. Grant had a couple of personal injury cases and a couple of paying hourly clients. We had a few thousand dollars saved, and he figured he could make it work."

"It seems to have worked out fine."

Samantha leaned back in her chair. "Grant always says that time was the best of his life. He made about half as much as he made at the big firm, but it seemed like the money went just as far. The kids were little, our overhead was practically nothing, and it seemed like there was a lot less pressure on both of us. Grant was happy. He didn't have many clients, but they appreciated his work, and he was proud to represent them."

"Has he always done medical malpractice cases?" Julie asked.

"Ever since he started."

"That looks like a tough business to me," said Julie. "Grant said it's probably going to cost more than fifty thousand dollars to run our case. How can he gamble that kind of money on a single case? And what happens when he loses one?"

"That's when it gets rough," Samantha said. "It's happened a couple of times. It happened in the last case he tried."

"Ouch."

"Ouch is right. But Grant looks at more than the money. He truly believes in his cases. He believes in yours." Samantha looked at Julie. "He also knows a lawsuit is a knife to the heart of any doctor, no matter who did what wrong. When your lawsuit is filed, Dr. Purser will take it personally. Anybody would."

Julie nodded, but her eyes let Samantha know she didn't exactly feel sorry for Purser.

"Grant makes sure he has good experts, and he always asks them to be critical about the case. If they have any doubts, he wants to know about it up front."

"It doesn't seem to bother him to go after the doctors," observed Julie.

"Oh, he worries about it now and then. I have an uncle who's a doctor, and he gives Grant the business about suing doctors. Some of the other parents from school and sports are doctors, or nurses, or they work for hospitals, and they give him a hard time, too. But I'll say this--Grant knows in his heart he's doing the right thing. If he loses a case, at least he did what he believed in."

"I'm glad he believes in our case," said Julie. "After the last couple of years, I need something to believe in myself."

# CHAPTER 15

Grant stepped into the master bathroom, weary from the struggle with his cuff links and resigned to asking his wife to help him get dressed. Samantha was in the final stage of hair and makeup, seated in her vanity chair wearing a sheer black silk robe and a smile. Without a word, she smoothed the crisp cotton cuffs, deftly slipped the silver and onyx links through the button holes, and stood to inspect his tie.

"How is it that you can tie a bow tie, but can't put in cuff links?" she asked.

"My wrists don't bend that way." Grant shrugged. "Besides, if you don't put in my cuff links, how will I get a look at you without your clothes on?"

Samantha tilted her head back to receive his kiss, wrapping her arms around his neck and pulling him tight.

"Get out of here so I can put on that dress," she protested, twisting playfully away from his attempt at another kiss. "We're late."

"True," admitted Grant. "But I'm glad you got to meet the Hallers today. Didn't I tell you they were nice people?"

"They're great," Samantha agreed. "Now scram."

Twenty minutes later, they were on their way to the Cattle Baron's Ball, an annual fundraiser at the Landmark Hotel in downtown Fort Worth. Grant hated formal fundraisers, though not because of the fundraising aspect. What bothered him was the one-upmanship of those in attendance. Each event brought out the new season's crop of trophy wives for the older gentlemen in the crowd, lower cuts in the evening gowns on the trophy wives, and flashier jewelry to complement the gowns.

The biggest show of the night came during the live auction, when local power brokers outbid each other for vacations, art, and sports memorabilia. While the winning bidder's funds went to the charity supported by the event, the purpose of the auction was far from philanthropic for most of the participants. The winner of each item could look around, especially at the runner-up, and give a smug nod that said, *Look at the scoreboard, pal. I have more money than you*. Grant knew that another such spectacle was in store for the evening, and that he would need to properly adjust his attitude.

The Mercers swept through the doors of the hotel, leaving the Tahoe entrusted to the valet service. Samantha was stunning in her own right, her black strapless gown cut deeply, but not immodestly low in the bust, fitted through the hips and waist, ending in flowing waves of black crepe trailing behind her as she moved. With each step, she revealed a black open-toed pump, with freshly pedicured toes and polished nails.

Grant surveyed the scene inside the ballroom door and had two thoughts. First, he believed that his wife was the most beautiful woman in the room. Second, he noticed that while the women all managed to have slightly different dresses, the men were all in the same basic outfit: black tuxedo, black shoes, white shirt, and black tie. He knew that a woman would be horrified to find another in her same dress at a formal event. Grant was relieved to find all the other men dressed exactly like him, for it meant that he hadn't made a fashion mistake.

After grabbing two glasses of wine, Grant took Samantha by the hand and led her through the crowd toward their table. A four-piece combo played in one corner of the cavernous ballroom, a decent rendition of *Just the Way You Look Tonight* emanating from their position.

The Mercers eventually found their table and slid into their chairs alongside Grant's partner, Charlie Montgomery, and his wife. The other six chairs were taken by clients of Montgomery's, along with their spouses, none of whom were terribly familiar to Grant. Idle conversation filled the first thirty minutes and was mercifully terminated when the meal was served. For hotel catering, the beef tenderloin was tasty and quite tender. Rosemary red potatoes and roasted vegetables were served alongside, also surprisingly delicious. A decent Merlot from the Monterey peninsula complemented the meal.

As dinner plates were removed and coffee served, the live auction began. No fireworks accompanied the first three items, but an audible buzz accompanied the announcement of the next item, a two-week vacation in a seven-bedroom house on Vail Mountain, including lift tickets and round-trip air travel in the homeowner's private jet. Grant watched with detached amusement as the bidding started at $25,000 and quickly escalated over $100,000. This narrowed the field of bidders from six to three to two in the space of ninety seconds. After another minute, the high bid stood at $200,000, and the auctioneer began the count.

"Going once," he intoned. "Going twice."

"TWO-FIFTY," shouted a newcomer to the proceedings.

"We have a new bid of $250,000. Do I hear three hundred?" When no response was heard, the auctioneer counted again. "Going once, going twice. Sold for $250,000. May I have the name of the winning bidder, please?"

"William Sellett," said the nearest spotter.

"I know that guy," said Grant. "He's the lobbyist for the tort reformers. Power broker in Austin, from what I hear."

"Mr. Sellett does a fine job for many of his clients, and the bills he helps with are beneficial to many of our own clients, Grant." Montgomery nodded in the direction of their guests.

Grant looked across the table and smiled. Two of their guests were high-ranking executives of insurance clients of the firm. Relieved he'd said nothing else, Grant simply smiled at Montgomery's comment, raising his glass and taking a full swallow of Merlot. "He's done a fine job, indeed."

Samantha cut a look at her husband and offered a slight smile. She pointed to her empty wine glass, giving Grant the chance to exit gracefully and avoid a potentially ugly conversation.

"More wine, anyone?" asked Grant as he rose from the table, turning without waiting for an answer.

"I'll come with you," said Samantha. She had to sprint to keep up with Grant, no easy feat in four-inch heels. When they got to the bar, she asked, "You okay?"

"Sure," said Grant. "You know how I am around those insurance types. They start talking politics, and it always turns out badly. I'll just stay away from the table, and stay away from politics while I'm there."

"Good boy," said Samantha. "I need you in a good mood tonight. You don't think I dressed up for all these other people, do you?"

Grant smiled at his wife and leaned down to give her a kiss. After handing her a glass of Chardonnay, he turned to head back toward the table and bumped directly into another patron of the ball, spilling his Merlot on the front of the man's tuxedo and the stiff white shirt underneath.

"Oh, my God, I'm so sorry," said Grant. "Let's get some club soda right away. And your next drink is on me."

"Don't worry about it," said the victim. "It's just a rental."

One look at the cut of the suit and the texture of the shirt told Grant this man would never wear a rented tuxedo. "That's nice of you," he said sheepishly, "but I know better about the tux. Please, let me buy you a drink."

"If you insist," said the gentleman. "My name's Bill Sellett."

"Grant Mercer," he said, shaking Sellett's extended hand. "Congratulations on the winning bid. Is there any room for more folks on the trip to Vail?"

"There might be." Sellett laughed. "But if we take you, we'll have to put down an extra deposit for the carpets."

Grant chuckled, too embarrassed to continue the banter about the ski trip. "Mr. Sellett, this is my wife, Samantha."

"It's a pleasure," said Sellett.

"Likewise," said Samantha, allowing Sellett to turn a handshake into a kiss to the back of her hand. "Such a gentleman."

"What'll it be, Mr. Sellett?" asked Grant.

"Macallan. Easy ice."

Grant turned, placed the order for the scotch and his replacement Merlot, and paid for the drinks. He turned again, carefully this time, and handed Sellett the highball glass and a clean bar rag provided by the waiter, along with a small bottle of club soda.

"If you'll get this on it now, you can probably keep a stain from setting in."

"Thanks, Grant. Samantha, will you hold this, please?" Sellett extended the scotch glass toward her.

"Let me have that instead," she said, taking the cloth and the club soda while handing her wine to Grant. She poured a small amount of the soda into the rag and dabbed at the front of Sellett's shirt. The red spot quickly turned to a light shade of pink and was hardly noticeable by the time Samantha finished her work. "All set."

"Thank you, Samantha. I guess I'll have to reconsider my decision on the trip to Vail."

"If you change your mind, just give Grant a call," she said.

As they walked away from the bar, Grant leaned over to Samantha. "Had enough of this for one night?"

"I thought you'd never ask."

# CHAPTER 16

With the Haller lawsuit about to be filed, Grant felt ready. He knew that the hardest part of a malpractice case came before the lawsuit was actually filed. Without maniacal preparation, even the best case could go sour.

Experts to defend doctors in such cases abounded, and a defense could always be mounted. It was usually just a matter of a slightly different interpretation of the medical record, or support from a relatively obscure journal article, to establish a credible defense. While the plaintiff bears the burden of proof, the defense need only establish doubt in the mind of the jurors to prevail. Grant had encountered this in nearly every case, and this one was no different.

Grant sent the required notice letter to Dr. Purser advising of the existence of the Hallers' claim and offering sixty days to settle. This was billed as the "opportunity to resolve the impending claim" in the table of contents of the statute, which always gave Grant a humorless laugh. Only once in nine years had he settled a case before suit was filed.

The claims adjuster assigned to Purser's case called about a week before the sixty days expired, asking whether Grant wanted to be reasonable and spare the family the heartache of litigation.

"That depends on your definition of reasonable," said Grant.

Without preface, the adjuster rolled out his usual speil. Grant had heard it so often, he actually lip synched along on the other end of the line. These are tough cases. Kids don't have an earnings history. It's sad, but all the money in the world won't bring back this child. Same load of crap, different case.

Grant listened for a minute, but quickly ran out of patience. "Save it, Frank," he said. "We both know this bullshit by heart, and I don't need to hear it again. You either pay the maximum or your man gets sued."

"I told you before," said the adjuster, "you won't get big money from me. Sue us. Take it to trial like you did in Middleton. Let's see if you can make it stick this time."

Grant banged the receiver down. Losing the Middleton trial had been a crippling blow, and the salt of the smug bastard's attitude stung what was still a remarkably fresh wound.

Grant swore under his breath, then made an oath of a different kind. He promised himself this case would be different.

# CHAPTER 17

Grant walked into Railhead BBQ and scanned the lunchtime crowd in search of Ed Haller. He was surprised to see that he had beaten Haller to their appointment. All it took was arriving ten minutes early.

Haller walked through the front door wearing a pair of khakis and a maroon golf shirt. In here, unlike most places, his flattop haircut made him look more like part of the regular crowd. Still, he cast an unmistakable aura of confidence and strength that easily distinguished Haller from everyone else.

"Let's get some grub, then we can talk for a while," Grant said while enduring a powerful handshake.

Grant slid his tray along the stainless steel rails of the serving line, choosing sliced brisket, pinto beans, and Cole slaw. Haller opted for smoked turkey, and the two men took their lunch to a table in the corner of the dining area, just beneath a neon Coors Light sign.

"What's on the agenda today, Mr. Mercer?" inquired Haller between bites of turkey.

"We've done your answers to their written questions," Grant said. "Now we get to do depositions. I'll take Purser's deposition first, but then we have to let them ask you and Julie questions. We need to spend some time getting you ready."

"Okay," said Haller. "Don't we need Julie with us for this?"

GREG McCARTHY

"Yes, but not yet. Sometimes it works better when we do the prep work separately." Grant chewed a bite of brisket. "They'll ask a bunch of questions about you. Where you grew up, college, military career, jobs, all that stuff. Let's just start with a dry run, let you talk about yourself a little."

"Not my favorite subject," Ed protested. "Nothing much to tell. College, Marine Corps, now here."

Grant leaned back in his chair and gathered his patience. "You can do better, Ed. I need details. Start from high school. Take me through your life."

"You know I hate this." Haller scowled. "I'm from Kerrville. My folks had a ranch outside town. After graduating from high school, I went to Texas A&M and joined the Corps. Not much doubt I'd do either. My dad and grandpa were both Aggies, and in those days there was no such thing as being an Aggie without being in the Corps."

"I had two friends from high school join the Corps at A&M," Grant said. "I'll tell you, I never understood it."

"Either you get it or you don't," Haller said with a shrug. "Anyway, I met Julie my senior year and had already signed up for four years with the Marines. So she and I dated long distance while she finished college and her Masters degree, then got married. Jennifer came along a couple years later, then Bradley after that."

"I know you had a career outside the military, too."

"Yeah, I did." Haller nodded. "I did my four years, then separated from the Marines and landed a job with an engineering firm in Fort Worth. I took that job so we could be close to Julie's parents out in Weatherford. Great job, too. Small firm, good guys. All Aggies, of course."

"Of course." Grant smiled.

80

"I was making pretty good money, and a year or two away from becoming a partner in the firm. Then came the September 11th attacks, and the whole world changed. I didn't mind going back to full-time duty, but I honestly never figured it would be for so long. You know, they promised us we'd only be on active duty for a year, then go back to our jobs and the reserves. I was also promised one tour in the Middle East, two at the most. I was on my fourth when this happened." Haller waved in the direction of his artificial leg.

"The extra tours must have been tough," said Grant quietly.

"Yeah," said Ed simply. "But not just for me. You know, when you leave on active duty, your employer doesn't have to keep paying you. I went from making nearly a hundred grand a year to collecting forty-five as a Marine Captain. We had just bought a house, so Julie had to get a job. She used to have one that paid more than mine, but she can't have a full-time job as a Human Resources manager and still take care of the kids. She took a teaching job paying next to nothing so she could be home with Jen and Bradley. She was unbelievable. Never complained."

That gave Grant the opportunity to shift the conversation where it needed to go. "Is Julie getting along any better these days?"

"Sometimes yes, sometimes no," mumbled Haller.

Grant saw once more that he would have to pull details out of Haller. "In what ways is she getting better?"

"With Bradley."

Grant waited a few seconds. "That's it?"

Haller Glared at Grant. "What do you want me to say?" he demanded. "She goes to more of Bradley's stuff than before."

"I'm sorry, Ed," Grant said as he put down his fork. "I know this is tedious. I know it's stupid to ask how your wife is doing after losing your daughter. I know. But we have to tell the jury how bad this is for both of you."

"Won't they already know?" Haller said. "How can they not know?"

"Nobody wants to lose a child, Ed. But every day, lots of people do. Those people hurt, they mourn, they recover, and they go on with their lives. Most of them never have to tell a group of twelve strangers about it and ask those strangers to give them money for their loss."

"I told you, I don't care about the money."

"You did. And I believe you. Like I said, it's all I can get for you. And the only way we get money is to be convincing to a jury. If you give one-word answers in court, the jury won't get to know who you are. If you give one-word answers in your deposition, then give nice, long answers in court, the jury will think you're playing a game, and they won't want to give you any money.

"Here's the other thing. This works best if you tell me about Julie and Julie tells me about you. That keeps it from looking like you're complaining, because juries don't like people who complain." Grant paused a moment. "Now, how's your wife doing?"

"She's still struggling," Ed said. "I see her becoming more involved with our son, Bradley, which is good, but she's still not the same. I don't think she ever will be."

"How is this affecting the relationship between the two of you?" asked Grant, moving to the least comfortable area of questioning right away.

"Now that's nobody's business," insisted Haller, pushing his chair back.

"Hold on, Ed. Usually it's not. But we're saying Jennifer's death has affected everything, including your relationship with each other."

"I don't like that. Julie won't like that."

"She already told me she doesn't like it, Ed. I never expected either of you to like it. But we still have to prepare for the depositions so we can keep putting pressure on the other side." Grant took a deep breath. "Again, how is this affecting you and your wife?"

Ed looked down at the half of his lunch that would go uneaten. "Can I talk to you man-to-man? Not to my lawyer?"

"Sure."

"Julie's crushed. It's been more than a year since Jen died, and it's like it happened yesterday. She's still different, and I don't think she'll ever be back to normal."

"Anything in particular giving you concern?"

"It's everything together," Haller said. She's withdrawn, she's depressed. She has no energy, and certainly none for me. When I come home, she barely acknowledges my presence."

"Have the two of you worked on your relationship?"

"If you're talking about our sex life, it barely exists. I was laid up for awhile, then Jen died. Neither of us felt like it for a long time. Julie still doesn't feel romantic or energetic, and I feel like a shit for bringing it up." Ed tilted back in his chair, letting out a frustrated sigh.

Grant let the silence linger for a moment, unsure of whether to push this issue today or just let Haller determine where the conversation would go. The problem solved itself quickly.

"There's something else, Mr. Mercer. Julie's smart. Probably too smart for her own good. She just keeps rolling this thing through her head, over and over. She clips articles out of magazines and the newspaper. She watches those shows like *Dateline*, looking for segments on children with cancer."

"That's normal, Ed," Grant said. "I've had dozens of clients call about research they've done on TV."

"That's not it," Ed said. "She's obsessed with the details. Hell, it's past the point of obsession. She's used the Internet to find out about the history of that law you told us about, to limit damages in these cases. She found the names of the legislators who sponsored the bill, and the names of the lobbyists who pushed for it. She found out who contributed to the campaigns of those guys in Austin. I had no idea there was so much money involved."

Grant nodded.

"And she didn't stop there. She showed me all about Castle Guard Insurance. Who runs the place, their balance sheet, premium collection numbers for the company, including what they take in from the military. She showed me everything."

"She hasn't given any of that stuff to me. Maybe it's just her way of trying to do something." Grant shrugged. "It can be an awfully helpless position, where you're supposed to leave everything to your lawyer."

"I didn't figure she'd talked to you about it," said Haller. "I keep telling her she needs to let you do your work, and there's nothing else we can do."

"What does she say to that?"

Haller sighed deeply, resting his chin on his fist. For the first time since they met, Grant could see the fatigue, the strain, and the pain on the face of his client. "She keeps saying it's not fair."

"She's right, you know," Grant said. "It's not."

"Yeah, I know." Haller looked at Grant, his steely eyes showing a fearful blend of fatigue and outrage. "It's not fair at all. See, Mr. Mercer, I'm used to things being fair. Not everything for everybody, of course, but mostly fair. That's why I joined the Marine Corps. We protect this country when we're called on, but we're also a pretty good tool for dispensing justice. Those terrorists came after us, over here, and they're paying the price. It has to be that way. You do something bad, you have to pay."

"We tried to tell people that when this tort reform bullshit came up," Grant said. "There were lots of people with lots of money on the other side, but most folks don't care until it affects them directly. We tried hard. We lost."

"Yeah," Haller muttered. "Who's losing now, Mr. Mercer?"

# CHAPTER 18

Soon after filing suit, Grant submitted his experts' reports. The first, from Dr. Howard, explained how Dr. Purser had been negligent for failing to order the CT scan. Dr. Perkins' report showed how Purser's error led directly to Jennifer Haller's death. Grant could finally confront Dr. Purser in person and get answers under oath about the decisions made and the reasons for making them.

For Grant, this was the best part of the system, but his clients universally misunderstood it. Most seemed to think the questioning could start immediately and go on indefinitely, with multiple opportunities to question each witness, especially the opposing party.

Medical malpractice cases had more limitations than other types of litigation, further complicating the situation. Grant could depose Purser only after filing his reports and, like other witnesses, the deposition could last no more than six hours. Still, no party could avoid being questioned. Scheduling was always a wrestling match and true cooperation was extraordinarily rare, but Purser eventually had to show up and answer questions about what he did.

Depositions in these cases posed a particular problem for Grant. Like most lawyers, he lacked a medical education. The people he deposed in these cases, on the other hand, were excellent students in college, studying mostly scientific subjects. They progressed to medical school, where they endured four more years of intense study. Internship and residency programs meant another four years in the crucible. Only then, in their early thirties and deeply in debt, did they emerge as full-fledged doctors, ready to enter practice and start working on patients without guidance. The disparity in the education and training between doctors and lawyers was stark, and frankly terrifying to Grant.

He made up the difference, as well as anyone could, through consultation with experts and hard work. In the weeks leading to Purser's deposition, Grant went to the medical school library at the University of Texas Southwestern Medical Center in Dallas at least a dozen times. He became a regular again, and it was telling that the reference librarians knew him by name.

Grant copied dozens of articles on pertinent medical issues and read them thoroughly. He made copies of the articles referenced in the previous set and read them, too. He made frequent calls to his experts to get their input on the issues addressed in the literature, and often got good leads from them on where to look for the latest articles.

Grant also made it a point to gain encyclopedic knowledge of his case, particularly the information in the medical records. He kept only a few cases on his docket an any given time because he knew that a high volume would erode his ability to familiarize himself with the details of each case, and would in turn make him a less effective advocate. This had caused its share of heartache at the firm, since the other lawyers billed by the hour and were dependent on a large volume of cases to generate the revenue necessary to keep profits at an acceptable level. Grant just put his head down, tuned out the frequent carping of his partners, and learned the medicine.

By the day of Purser's deposition, Grant was ready. After they exchanged pleasantries, Purser took the oath, and Grant dove right in.

"Dr. Purser, please tell me why you decided not to order a CT scan on Jennifer Haller after her first visit to your office."

Purser clearly wasn't expecting this. Grant knew that most lawyers spend at least two hours on preliminaries, which let the witness get comfortable and have the facts of the case straight in his own mind before the tougher questions came. He'd counted on the surprise to disorient Purser.

"Um, well," Purser stammered, "there are a great many reasons she didn't have a CT scan, but I didn't decide not to order one."

"That's what I want to know, doctor," Grant said. "Please tell me why you didn't order the CT. That was a conscious decision on your part, was it not?"

Grant secretly delighted in Purser's dilemma. Neither answer was good. If Purser admitted to a conscious decision-making process, he had to say that the failure to order the CT scan was a choice. If, on the other hand, he said that the lack of a CT scan wasn't a choice, it became an oversight. Purser certainly didn't want to admit that.

"Again," said Purser, "I didn't decide that she shouldn't have a CT scan. Rather, I assessed the patient and didn't believe, based on her clinical presentation, that a CT scan was required at that time."

"What was your diagnosis when you first saw Jennifer?" asked Grant.

"When I first saw Miss Haller, I suspected she had either cluster or migraine headaches. The other possibilities were TMJ and stress-related headache."

"Was that the extent of your differential diagnosis?"

Purser paused a moment, then replied, "Yes, it was."

Grant pressed. "Why didn't you consider a tumor as part of your differential diagnosis?"

Doctors are trained to make a list of the potential illnesses or injuries in their patients, ranked from highest probability to lowest. This differential diagnosis system is the basis for examinations and tests designed to rule out the possibilities one by one, until there are only one or two items on the list. Unfortunately for Purser, he'd noted his differential diagnosis in Jennifer's chart, and a brain tumor was nowhere on the list.

"That's easy to do in hindsight, Mr. Mercer, but the presence of a tumor was felt to be only a remote possibility," Purser explained. "I felt we had enough time to see if the symptoms would simply go away."

"Would you agree with me that brain tumors are the leading cause of unresolved headaches lasting more than two weeks in children under the age of twelve?" This was the conclusion of the latest article on the subject, published in the prestigious *New England Journal of Medicine*.

Purser had no choice. "Yes."

"And would you agree that when the headaches are accompanied by nausea and vomiting, also lasting for more than two weeks, a brain tumor should be the number one item on a differential diagnosis?"

"Yes," Purser said, staring at the luxurious carpet beneath his feet.

"If you knew that, why didn't you include a brain tumor in your differential diagnosis of Jennifer Haller." Grant knew he had accomplished what he had come to do.

"I just didn't think she had a brain tumor," said Purser. "You make it sound like we're supposed to know everything all the time. This isn't a cooking class, where I open the book and follow a recipe and everything's fine. We're talking about the possibility of cutting opening a little girl's head when all she had wrong with her was a bad head cold."

"How many other patients of yours have died from a bad head cold?" asked Grant, unable to resist the temptation.

"Objection," hollered Purser's lawyer. "Counsel, you need to ask legitimate questions and stop harassing the doctor, or we're out of here."

"I didn't bring up the subject of head colds, but we'll move on for now," said Grant, casting a thin smile in the direction of Dr. Purser.

Grant spent the next four hours confirming more details from the chart, hitting the high points of the medical literature, and quizzing Purser about the other members of his group who might know anything about the case.

After crossing off the last item on his checklist, Grant leaned toward the doctor and locked eyes. In a soft voice he asked, "What do you think would be a fair resolution to this case, doctor? How much do you think this child's life was worth?"

"Don't answer that question," thundered Purser's lawyer.

"He can if he wants," said Grant.

"This deposition is over," bellowed the defense lawyer. "Let's go, doctor."

"Wrong, counselor," said Grant without shifting his glare from Purser. "This case is over."

# CHAPTER 19

The depositions of Ed and Julie Haller went well, though the emotional toll was significant. Julie led off, since she was the one who took Jen to the doctors and was the historian for the case.

Grant had a good feeling about the depositions of his clients, which was rare. Depositions aren't usually won by the witness. The process wasn't designed to let a witness shine or to tell his story, but instead to allow questioning by lawyers. Most of Grant's clients weren't gifted speakers, and many prattled on endlessly despite his admonitions to answer the questions and otherwise be quiet. Grant was always careful to tell his clients not to expect too much out of their deposition, and that they would probably feel extremely frustrated.

The Hallers, however, presented a different look. Both Ed and Julie were educated, and were used to communicating with others on a mutually understandable level. Julie Haller had worked for a couple of Fortune 500 companies before electing to stay home to raise a family. She was attractive in a non-threatening way, with an air about her that put people at ease.

Unlike most of Grant's clients, Julie Haller had the experience of sending a husband to a foreign war zone on multiple occasions and helping that husband recover from an amputation on his return home.

After such an experience, it was hard to see how a lawyer would intimidate her. In short, Grant considered her to be the perfect client.

Grant had spent hours preparing Julie for her deposition, and had warned her about questions that in ordinary conversation would be rude at best. He'd cautioned her to keep in mind that depositions were a necessary evil, and that this wasn't the time for her to try to convince anyone of anything. Still, he knew these depositions could make or break the case.

Purser's attorney was T. Scott Wynn, a ten-year lawyer who'd recently been promoted to partner at the relatively small Dallas firm of Gates & Riley. Wynn was pudgy and wore his hair short on the sides and longer on top. The effect was to accentuate the roundness of his face, especially considering the muffin top protruding over his shirt collar. The French blue shirt was expensive, however, and displayed Wynn's initials on each white cuff. Gold cuff links matched the collar bar, which held the white collar of the shirt tightly to Wynn's fleshy neck under a hideous Paisley tie. Grant sat between Ed and Julie Haller in a pair of slacks and a golf shirt.

Wynn first took Julie through about an hour of questions about her life, as far back as junior high school and up to the present. Throughout, Wynn acted as though his natural charm, or at least his designer haircut and excessive Polo cologne, would make Julie feel grateful for the experience.

Naturally, Wynn wanted to take as much time as possible, since he and his firm were being paid by the hour. The method had been described by one of Grant's experts as a defense lawyer's attempt to recognize the full economic benefit of the file. Others referred to it as gouging. Either way, it was disgraceful when applied to the deposition of the mother of a dead little girl.

He inquired in full detail about her family, brothers and sisters, medical background, education, work history, and her marriage to Captain Ed Haller. Wynn asked whether she'd ever been convicted of a felony, whether she'd ever smoked marijuana, and whether she and her husband had ever been separated since the date of their wedding.

"You mean other than the times when the Marines sent him to the Middle East to fight? No, never been separated other than that."

Grant couldn't tell which he liked better, the answer or the look of horror on the face of T. Scott Wynn when she delivered it.

Once Wynn finished with the warm-ups, he asked Julie about Jennifer's medical condition before the headaches started. Julie confirmed the information in the medical records of her daughter's doctors. Jennifer had been a completely normal child with the usual illnesses and nothing else. No complications in the pregnancy or delivery, no injuries during her childhood, and no reason to believe she had anything wrong with her until the headaches began.

"What made you take her to the doctor in the first place, Mrs. Haller?" Wynn asked.

"Jen had occasional headaches for a few months," Julie explained. "When they started to get more frequent, I thought I should take her in."

"But your pediatrician apparently told you he suspected nothing serious and gave your daughter only prescription strength ibuprofen and a muscle relaxant, correct?"

"That's right," Julie said.

"And your pediatrician never ordered or suggested a CT scan, did he?" Wynn asked.

"He did not."

"Did you ever ask him to do a CT on your daughter?"

"Yes, I did. That's when he sent me to your client," Julie said.

"When your daughter saw Dr. Purser for the first time, did you tell him you wanted him to order a CT scan?" Wynn asked.

"Yes, I did."

"Can you explain why the records from my client's office have nothing in them reflecting a request from you for a CT scan?" Wynn leaned forward, apparently expecting a simple *no*.

"If you're asking me whether I ever wrote a letter to Dr. Purser demanding that my daughter have her head x-rayed to check for a tumor, the answer is that I did not," Julie said coolly. "If you're asking why Dr. Purser failed to write a single word in his notes about our long conversation concerning CT scans and my desire to have one ordered for my daughter, the only explanation I have is that his records have been carefully drafted to cover his own ass."

Grant's chest swelled with pride.

"If that was the purpose," Wynn countered, "why wouldn't Dr. Purser just order the CT? He wasn't going to pay for it, and it certainly wasn't a test that would hurt your daughter or pose any significant risk. Why not just order the CT?"

"He's the doctor, Mr. Wynn," Julie said. "I trusted him with my daughter's life, and he let me down. I'd tell you to ask your client yourself, but I've read his deposition, and he didn't have an answer to that question when he was under oath. I guess we'll never have one."

Wynn flinched, then took a break in the deposition. As a partner in the firm, he habitually left the defense of his clients' depositions to younger associates. In this case, the task had fallen to Coleman Farrigut, a recent hire who'd spent the first two years of his career clerking for the Texas Supreme Court.

Unfortunately, Farrigut had no idea what he was doing when not reading cases or writing briefs, and he simply hadn't prepared Dr.

Purser as well as he should have. Wynn had skimmed the transcript, but hadn't read it thoroughly. He was totally blindsided. Coleman Farrigut would get his ass chewed, but the damage was done.

After the break, Wynn returned to the deposition of Julie Haller with far less enthusiasm. He walked her through the remainder of the medical care received by Jennifer from the time of her diagnosis to her death, taking care to get information about the treatment without asking Julie to describe in detail the effects on her daughter and family. Julie held up well for the most part, faltering only when asked to describe how Jennifer's death had affected her husband.

Grant knew that Wynn hated this part of depositions like this, not because he was concerned about the people he deposed, but because there was nothing to gain from making Julie Haller uncomfortable. It would just make him look like a bully, which was something Wynn couldn't afford with a witness like this. Wynn still had to depose the Ed Haller, whose eyes remained fixed on Wynn during Julie's deposition.

Occasionally, Grant caught Wynn looking nervously in Haller's direction. Beads of sweat formed on his upper lip, betraying the fear generated by Haller's steady glare. Grant smiled inwardly at the realization that Wynn was thoroughly intimidated and probably worried that Haller would kick his ass, prosthetic leg or not.

# CHAPTER 20

After a late lunch, Ed Haller's deposition went smoothly; though much shorter than his wife's, owing mostly to the fact that T. Scott Wynn experienced difficulty breathing throughout the afternoon. Haller related his own family history, educational experiences, and the highlights of his career as a Marine officer. Wynn wanted to spend more time on Haller's injury in Iraq and the loss of his leg.

"I hope you don't mind, Captain Haller," Wynn said, "but I need to ask you some questions about the loss of your leg and how it's affected you."

"Certainly." Grant's request for short answers had been wasted on Haller. For a Marine, any sort of interrogation, especially formal ones with court reporters and oaths, was a situation suited to as little talk as possible.

"Do you have more than one prosthesis?" Wynn asked.

"Yes, sir."

"Please tell me about the artificial legs you have, what purpose they serve, and where you got them."

"I have the prosthesis I'm wearing right now, which is controlled with a computer chip to make the movement of the leg and foot as natural as possible. It's a transfemoral prosthesis, which means that my leg was amputated above the knee. It's made of titanium and must be removed for me to swim, shower, or bathe.

"I have another prosthesis built for running, with a flexible carbon composite blade for a foot. That leg enables me to run, although it's not as stable or natural as this leg. It's obviously not as natural looking.

"I'm scheduled to be fitted soon for a third prosthesis, one designed to withstand water and the elements. Its motors, sensors, and computers are sealed, so I can bathe, shower, and swim with the leg attached, rather than having to do those things with only my remaining leg.

"All of these prostheses came from the Center for the Intrepid at Brooke Army Medical Center at Fort Sam Houston, in San Antonio, Texas."

"Tell me about that," said Wynn.

Haller spent the next few minutes telling Wynn how the Fallen Heroes Fund, a private non-profit organization dedicated to supporting soldiers who suffer catastrophic injuries in the wars in Iraq and Afghanistan, their families, and the families of soldiers killed in the line of duty. The organizers saw the need for such a program when they observed the delay and denial caused by government red tape, particularly from the Veteran's Administration, when it came to medical treatment of injured war veterans. In the first few years of its existence, the fund had raised and distributed more than sixty million dollars.

"The Center for the Intrepid houses rehabilitation equipment and personnel," continued Haller, "and has the best prosthetic program in the world. They train us and our wives about how to take care of our prosthesis, and they have a place for our families to stay while they're down there."

"Do they provide counseling assistance as well, Captain?"

Haller fidgeted. "They do."

"Have you made use of those counseling services?"

"I have," Haller said.

"Have any of the doctors or counselors you've seen diagnosed you with depression or post traumatic stress disorder?" Wynn asked.

"Yes, sir." Haller wanted to look at Grant, but resisted.

"And are you still being treated for those conditions?"

"Yes, sir."

Although he was tempted, Haller remembered Grant's advice to answer only the question asked. He wanted to explain to this weasel that the depression and post traumatic stress were due in part to his leg, in part to the death of so many of his Marine comrades, and in part to the sense of frustration he felt over the war as a whole.

Haller wanted to tell him that he never wanted to go to Iraq, but did his duty when sent because Saddam Hussein had to be removed from power, and weapons of mass destruction had to be found and dismantled. He wanted to scream at this pale, flabby excuse of a man that he returned to Iraq for his second, third, and fourth tours of duty in spite of the fact that he now knew that he and the rest of the military had been deceived, that there were no weapons of mass destruction and never had been.

He wanted to convey in short and simple terms that he felt used by a government spending a trillion dollars on a war in a country half a world away, and another trillion to rebuild what they destroyed, money given to American contractors with business ties to politicians. Haller wanted to grab the lawyer by his monogrammed shirt and explain to him that he felt betrayed by a government that would send him and thousands of other soldiers to war with inferior equipment to save a few bucks in the military budget, then provide inadequate medical care for wounds that could have been prevented with better equipment.

He wanted to express to T. Scott Wynn his disbelief at the government's refusal to provide top-quality prosthetics to amputee veterans, and his disgust that so many veterans with mental illness went entirely untreated after their separation from military service.

"Yeah," Haller longed to say, "I suffer from depression and stress because of the shit I've been through. I'm screwed up in the head after watching fellow Marines killed and maimed. I'm a little unbalanced after being sent to the Middle East to fight four times in three years. Wouldn't you be a little fucked up, too?"

Instead, Haller simply said, "Yes, sir."

The rest of the deposition went much the same, with Haller giving short, terse answers to the questions posed by T. Scott Wynn. Haller's calm and polite demeanor belied the turbulence churning just beneath the surface.

# CHAPTER 21

Bill Sellett found himself gearing up for another legislative session. His usual method was to operate behind the scenes, leaving the limelight and publicity to others. This time, however, he took a different tack, playing the front man in the efforts to influence public opinion on the issue of tort reform. Sellett's assignment was to use his charm, influence, and access to the offshore accounts of his clients to change the hearts and minds of legislators.

For months, Sellett had been schmoozing these public servants. Fortunately, many of the legislators had business in Austin even when the legislature wasn't in session, and he spent a substantial amount of time entertaining in his adopted hometown, where the variety of entertainment and dining options was practically infinite. A Driftwood smokehouse known as The Salt Lick, about thirty minutes from Sellett's office, was a favorite among several of the legislators and their staffers. On any given day, customized Harleys outnumbered cars and trucks in the parking lot, and the beef brisket, served with a healthy slathering of mustard-based sauce, was worth the trip.

Sellett sat enjoying the Salt Lick ribs and brisket combo plate with a client from Hartford when he was approached by Nate Harris, a staffer for State Senator Ken Dunbar. After introductions by Sellett, Harris leaned a bit closer to Sellett.

"Sorry to bring this up now, but I imagine you heard about Senator Dunbar."

"I did," Sellett replied. "Do the police have any leads?"

"Not as far as I know," Harris said, "but I'm checking in constantly with the sheriff and with the FBI."

"I sure hope they can get something done. I worked with Senator Dunbar pretty closely on the med mal reforms and had tremendous respect for him. How's his family?"

"Holding up pretty well, under the circumstances."

"Well, give them my regards," Sellett said. "Let's get together in the next few days to talk about what you're planning on doing in the future."

"Will do," said Harris as he headed for the door.

"What was that about?" asked Sellett's client.

"A state senator was murdered last weekend near his vacation home about three hours north of here. Nobody can think of a reason, and the cops have no leads." Sellett shook his head. "Real shame, too. He was a nice guy."

"No leads at all?" asked the client. "That seems strange."

"Nobody knows of any enemies of the senator," Sellett said with another shake of the head. "He was a politician and had opponents, but he never stepped on anybody's toes. Like I said, everyone is a bit lost on this."

"Well, let's hope they can figure something out."

As the two men finished their supper, another customer sat quietly in corner of the patio, casually gnawing on a smoked pork rib through a neat beard and mustache. Sellett and his client stayed and talked for a half hour after they'd finished eating, sipping bottled beer. The bearded stranger peered out from under the brim of a Texas Longhorns hat, watching their every move.

# Chapter 22

Bill Sellett and his latest girlfriend, Abigail Connors, enjoyed a casual dinner with Nate Harris and his wife at the Cedar House, a popular new spot near downtown Austin overlooking Town Lake.

"I was pretty upset when I first heard the news," Sellett said, his voice low. "Ken was a friend of mine."

"I remember seeing you at a couple of football games together." Harris nodded.

"Yeah," muttered Sellett. He drew a breath, sat up straight, and scrutinized the smoky depths of his scotch before draining the glass. "We also worked on several pieces of legislation together. That's how I got to know him. We were busy on some insurance bill, and started talking about boats. He and his wife came out with me on my Cobalt for the weekend and just had a blast."

Sellett's gaze drifted away as he spoke, and in his mind he pictured the glittering waters of Lake Travis, which had been their personal playground on that glorious afternoon.

"The boat trip got me an invitation to Possum Kingdom. Have you been to his house there?"

"Afraid not," lamented Harris. "We were supposed to visit the weekend after the senator was killed."

"Well," Sellett said, "you missed it. I've seen some great places in my day, but this thing blew me away. It's an honest-to-God log cabin, inside and out. Leather sofas and chairs, wrought iron everywhere, rough cedar for all the cabinets and beams. It's huge, but feels real cozy.

"And you should see the animals in there. It's a taxidermist's dream. There's a buffalo head over the mantle, elk and deer heads everywhere, even a full-body coyote on top of the kitchen cabinet. You have to see this place to believe it."

"I guess that won't happen now," Harris said.

An awkward moment followed before Sellett could stand it no longer. "Anything new on the investigation?"

"Still nothing." Harris shook his head. "No prints on the car. No hair, blood, or anything that could be tested for DNA. No fibers. Hell, no murder weapon. They know it was a knife, and probably a big one. The wound nearly decapitated him.

"Nobody saw anyone with the senator that day. A store clerk said he came in alone, spent about fifteen minutes shopping, and left by himself. Nobody noticed anything in the parking lot or on the road, but there weren't many people at the lake that weekend anyway."

"Did the feds talk to you?" asked Sellett.

"Yeah, twice," replied Harris. "The first time, it was like an inquisition. I think they probably treated everyone the same, but I felt like a suspect. They kept asking me where I was and what I knew about the senator's whereabouts. I think they must have crossed me off the list, because the next time they wanted to know about the senator's business and political career. They kept asking me about his enemies, although they didn't seem to believe me when I told him I didn't know of any. They even went into opponents on legislation."

"What did you tell them about that?" Sellett asked.

"There's not much to tell. Hell, the legislature's so Republican there were practically no opponents. Other than that mess about the lake, he never stirred up controversy. I honestly couldn't name one person who had it in for him politically." Harris paused for a moment, then asked, "What's the best thing he did in the Senate?"

Sellett leaned back, gently rocking his fresh glass of scotch. "I remember being amazed at his ability to push the tort reform bills through without alienating everybody on the other side of the issue. Of course, there really wasn't anybody on the other side of that fight in those days. At least not anybody with any money or political clout."

This brought a crooked smile to Harris' face. "That's true. The trial lawyers gave it a run, but it was no contest. Your people had too much money, better advertisements, and you." Harris lifted his martini in a toast.

Sellett clinked his scotch glass in appreciation. This was a true compliment from somebody who was keenly aware of the importance of a skilled lobbyist, and nothing made Sellett as happy as hearing such a compliment. Well, almost nothing. A quick glance across the corner of the table at the striking young Miss Abigail Connors reminded Sellett that happiness had categories, and some categories just naturally carry more weight than others.

Sellett's mind wandered back to the first time they'd been together. They'd spent the night at his house in Westlake Hills. The back deck, with its hot tub and fantastic view of the city skyline, was the perfect setting for their initial tryst. Afterward, they'd crashed in his king-sized bed, totally exhausted.

Abigail had needed only a short nap before reaching over to fondle him into a state where he could be of use to her once again. After a second session, she'd awakened him during the night, again demanding satisfaction. Though he'd been happy to please her again, he'd been exhausted for the next three days and vowed that they would henceforth rendezvous at her place, where he could excuse himself and return home for blessed rest.

They wrapped up dinner and slid into Sellett's Mercedes for the short trip to Abigail's apartment. Sellett didn't think he had the patience for the ten-minute drive. Abigail had no intention of making him wait.

Sellett stayed until one-thirty. He gave her a kiss on the neck, apologized for being unable to stay the night, and quietly dressed. Abigail protested mildly, which always made Sellett feel better, but he wondered whether the newness was wearing off for her. He decided he'd stay the night next time and move the relationship to the next level. Abigail might be the one.

Sellett sank into the rich leather of the driver's seat of the Benz, once again overcome with the feeling of complete satisfaction. As he pulled out of the parking lot, the Harmon-Kardon sound system pumped the soundtrack of his life through its fourteen speakers, the Eagles filling the space with the strains of *Peaceful Easy Feeling*.

# CHAPTER 23

Sellett eased the Mercedes into his driveway, the automatic gate closing behind him. The prowler ducked between the sections of wrought iron just before it closed and walked quickly along the edge of the Pavestone drive, careful to stay more in the shadows than in the light. The intruder stepped undetected through the breezeway toward the side door of Sellett's home wearing a baseball cap pulled down low and a graying beard of about two weeks' growth. A baggy hooded sweatshirt sported a Gothic print message on the front.

When Sellett emerged from the garage the stranger took two explosive strides and slammed an aluminum baseball bat into Sellett's ribs, knocking the breath from his lungs. Another swing of the bat broke Sellett's left wrist when he raised his hands to defend himself.

Sellett fell backward, his head snapping back against the wood walkway between the house and garage. The attacker moved quickly, landing on Sellett's chest, pinning his arms to the deck under both legs. Sellett flailed both hands and drove his knees upward, searching for a soft and vulnerable spot. He found none.

Sellett swung both hands around the arms of his opponent and grabbed for the face. When his right hand found a cheek, half of his assailant's beard was suddenly gone. As Sellett stared wide-eyed at the handful of short hair, his attacker pulled a Bowie knife from its sheath and drew the razor-sharp blade across Sellett's throat. Sellett stopped struggling in an instant as blood surged from the wound.

The killer quickly pulled the wristwatch from Sellett's wrist and examined it, hoping someone would remember that Sellett owned a collection of expensive timepieces, including this Patek Phillipe. It would be in a convenience store trash can by sunrise, but it would be an important part of the effort to mislead the police. For the same reason, Sellett's wallet was removed from the pocket of his trousers. The vinyl gloves made it a bit awkward to sort through the wallet, but the killer managed to pull out the cash, about $800 for a quick guess, and flip through the rest of the wallet's contents. The credit cards would be discarded later without actually using them. The cash would go, too. This wasn't about money.

A final glance around the area revealed nothing out of the ordinary, other than a dead lawyer clutching a handful of hair in his right hand. The killer bent down, opened the hand, and retrieved the false beard, which had been purchased the previous month in a costume shop.

"Goodbye, Mr. Sellett."

It was two blocks to the truck, and a couple of hours of driving before sleep could be found, but fatigue wasn't a problem. To the contrary, there was a certain energized feeling, born of the knowledge that this mission was proceeding exactly as planned.

# CHAPTER 24

"Impressive, isn't it?"

The voice of Dr. Fredrick Howard startled Grant as he took in the view of Mt. Rainier from the ten-foot windows on the eighth floor of the medical center at the University of Washington.

"Stunning," Grant agreed while shaking Howard's hand. "It looks like it's right outside, but it's fifty miles from here."

"More like sixty. Ever get up there?"

"To the park about halfway," Grant said. "My uncle and cousin invited me to climb it with them about ten years ago, but I passed. Too busy."

"You'll have the chance again," Howard said. "I didn't know you had family here."

"Aunt, uncle, and three cousins on my mom's side. We get up here every two or three years to see them. We don't have things like that in Texas." Grant gestured out the window toward the snow-capped flattop of Rainier's peak, regretting his missed opportunity to climb it.

"You also don't have golf in July without sweating through two shirts, do you?" asked Howard with a grin.

"I see you've been to our state."

"I was a guest of Uncle Sam at Fort Hood in fabulous Killeen, Texas."

"This shouldn't be so bad today," Grant said as they sat. "Have you ever met T. Scott Wynn?"

"Never had the pleasure."

"He's about what you'd expect. We'll be here awhile. He'd like to stay late enough not to have to catch a flight out until tomorrow. And he'll be about as pleasant as a pit bull with a toothache."

"No problem." Howard shrugged. "I've set aside the whole afternoon. Besides, I've tangled with dozens of those lawyers. They all go by the same playbook. He'll ask about my fees, about how we met, all about our conversations, right?"

Grant nodded.

"He'll spend an hour on my résumé and he'll have me agree that a bad result doesn't necessarily mean malpractice."

The two men spent the next half hour discussing Jennifer's case. Grant played the part of opposing counsel, stopping occasionally to review a part of the medical record. Grant felt good about Howard's preparation and anticipated no problems.

Wynn predictably burned a couple of hours at the outset with questions that would have fit nicely into about ten minutes, then got to the heart of his interrogation.

"Just so we're clear, you're being paid for your opinions in this case, isn't that right?"

"Absolutely not," Howard replied. "My opinions are not for sale."

"You're not doing this for free, though," Wynn shot back. "Mr. Mercer is paying you to work on this case, isn't he?"

"Just like you're being paid by Dr. Purser's insurance company."

"I'll bet your rates are a lot higher than mine," Wynn said with a smirk.

"I'll bet you're right," Howard said. "I assume you'll get paid whether your client wins this case or not."

"As will you."

"True," Howard agreed. "The difference is that I wouldn't have worked on this case if I didn't believe your client killed Jennifer Haller. I doubt that makes any difference to you."

This stopped the exchange momentarily, and Wynn decided to change tactics.

"All right, Dr. Howard, why don't we start with this." Wynn's tone now conveyed that he would like to have a polite professional discussion. "Please tell me why you think my client was negligent in his treatment of Jennifer Haller."

Howard cleared his throat. "First, I believe Dr. Purser admitted as much in his deposition when he told Mr. Mercer that he didn't include a brain tumor in his differential diagnosis. Of equal importance, he failed to make the proper assessment of his patient and failed to utilize the diagnostic tests available to him to locate the tumor in her head. The standard of care requires a physician in the situation presented to Dr. Purser to make a full and proper differential diagnosis, which in this case must include a brain mass. Dr. Purser failed to take advantage of all available methods of ruling out that possibility before making another diagnosis."

"Do you agree that Jennifer Haller's symptoms are not exclusively caused by brain tumors, and could have been the result of several different disease processes?" asked Wynn. This was the heart of the defense of the case.

"Sure."

"Then explain to me how it was negligent for him to consider these other disease processes as the cause of the symptoms."

THE PRICE OF LIFE

"I feel sure you understand the distinction, Mr. Wynn, but it wasn't negligent for him to consider the others. It was negligent for him not to have a brain tumor at or near the top of the list."

"But wasn't it far more likely that allergies, a low-grade infection, or stress was causing her headaches?"

Howard knew this was true, but only when taken out of context. "If you're asking for pure percentages, I would agree," he said. "But the important thing in assessing a patient using a differential diagnosis is to consider the severity of the conditions and the risk of failing to detect them.

"If she had allergies that went untreated, she'd continue to suffer allergy symptoms. Her body would probably have fought off a low-grade infection, and a course of antibiotics could have been prescribed any time. But an undiagnosed brain tumor can be fatal in children, and in fact usually is. Dr. Purser seems to have simply ignored this when he saw Jennifer Haller."

"Even if he had sent her for a CT scan, you can't really say she would have survived for sure, can you?"

"I'm familiar with the literature, and I know that an astrocytoma is considered highly survivable if diagnosed at a certain stage, but I'm not regularly involved in the treatment of these tumors. I would defer to Dr. Perkins on that issue."

"Would you defer to any doctor who has been regularly involved in the treatment of those tumors?" Wynn probed a potential weakness.

"Generally, no," Howard said. "I usually don't defer on opinions on complex medical issues unless I'm familiar with a doctor's credentials and experience. In this case, I happen to know Dr. Perkins quite well and have referred patients to him for the new laser surgery he's working on in San Antonio."

Wynn seemed mildly disappointed in the answer.

"What about our expert in this case, Dr. Fletcher from Bellevue?" Wynn inquired. "You know him, don't you?"

"I certainly do, and I respect his opinion. But in this case, I wouldn't defer to him. His program does great work, but they haven't made the same progress made by Dr. Perkins and his staff. So while he's entitled to his opinion and I respect him, I believe Dr. Perkins is in a much better position to give the best opinion about the chances of saving Jennifer's life."

"But you worked with Dr. Fletcher for four years in the neurology and neurosurgery program at Bellevue, didn't you?" Wynn had now hit the single soft spot in Howard's armor—his close association with the lead expert witness for the defense.

"I did indeed."

Wynn's eyes flashed and he bored in hard. "You and Dr. Fletcher authored several articles together on the subject of surgery to remove brain tumors, isn't that correct?"

"We did," Howard said while keeping a placid expression.

"Does Dr. Fletcher have less experience in this field than Dr. Perkins?"

"No."

"Then how can you claim that Dr. Perkins has better answers? How can you be sure this little girl's life would have been spared?" Wynn asked. There was simply no way any doctor could testify he was sure about anything. All the law required was reasonable probability, but doctors were more accustomed to needing virtual perfection, and the question of certainty usually did the trick in an expert's deposition.

Howard smiled at Wynn. "Because I talked to Dr. Perkins just last week. I reviewed the records from the last twelve patients in his trial of the laser procedure. All twelve of those patients survived, their

THE PRICE OF LIFE

tumors were completely removed, and none suffered any complications. In language you would understand, Mr. Wynn, the laser surgery works. And it works every time."

Wynn was clearly stunned. No literature had yet been published about Perkins' program. "And you rely only on your discussions with Dr. Perkins for this?"

"Not at all," Howard said. "I just told you that in addition to talking with Dr. Perkins, I reviewed the medical records of the patients who underwent the procedure. What I didn't tell you was that I had the privilege of observing surgery last week in San Antonio, and talking to the patient before and after the procedure." Howard winked at Grant as he spoke. It was Grant's turn to be stunned. Howard hadn't mentioned this little nugget in their meeting.

"All of this information will be made available to me, of course," stammered Wynn in Grant's general direction.

"Absolutely," Grant said.

Grant had always loved Seattle, but the place had just shot to the top of his list of favorites.

# CHAPTER 25

Sheriff Ronnie Clyde Barlow sipped strong black coffee and munched absently on a strip of bacon and a homemade cinnamon roll while getting his weekly sports fix from the Sunday edition of the *Fort Worth Star Telegram*. It was just past eight on a Sunday morning, and sunlight lay across the breakfast table in bright ribbons, alternating with dark shadows cast by the half-open window blinds. While Barlow spent his usual thirty minutes with the Sports section, his wife read the entire paper, then puttered around the kitchen picking up dishes and beginning preparations for the day's afternoon meal. Barlow picked up the Regional section and read the lead story above the fold:

> *William Sellett, a lawyer with the firm of Rayburn Williams & Dodd, was found dead yesterday outside his Westlake Hills home. Sellett, 45, had lived in Austin since 2000, when he founded the Austin office of the Washington law firm. A police source confirmed that they are treating the matter as a homicide, but declined to release any information about cause of death. The source also stated that Sellett had been with friends during the evening, but that the friends had been questioned and eliminated as suspects.*

*Sellett was closely involved with legislative efforts on behalf of the insurance industry and several major corporations during the eight years he lived in Austin. Associates say he was instrumental in the passage of recent tort reforms, including the passage of a constitutional amendment capping recovery by plaintiffs in medical malpractice cases.*

*Austin Police said the investigation was continuing, although a spokesman declined to offer more specifics.*

Barlow read the article again before his mind registered the gnawing feeling at the base of his head. He told his wife he'd be back in a little while and headed out the door. Five minutes later, he was behind the desk at his office, sifting through the case file on the murder of Senator Ken Dunbar.

He found what he was looking for in the senator's official bio, which listed his positions and accomplishments as a member of the Texas legislature. Page four of the bio noted that the senator had chaired the Committee on Civil Justice. Under that bullet point, the bio pointed out that the senator led the effort to pass several tort reform packages, including caps on medical malpractice cases.

Barlow's neck started to tingle. Two victims of violent deaths, less than three weeks apart. Both men prominent figures in the legislature, connected by a controversial and high-profile legislative effort. The sheriff decided this was something he needed to share with the Federal Bureau of Investigation. If they could just forget about who got credit and take advantage of the information he could provide them, they might even solve the case.

Before he saw the feds, though, he needed to run a few traps. He called his wife and told her he'd be working all afternoon but would be home by dinner. He then climbed in his Chevy Blazer and took off toward the lake. He knew Sunday would be a good time to catch a few permanent lake residents, many of whom worked in the restaurants, shops, and marinas, where weekends provided the majority of revenue for the season.

His first stop was Stumpy's, the barbeque joint and lake institution. Jack "Stumpy" LeGrande, a transplanted Texan by way of the swamps of western Louisiana, was a fixture in the lake community and the best source of information in the county, bar none. Stumpy stood all of five foot five on his best day, making the origin of his nickname completely obvious. His face was littered with salt and pepper whiskers after a week without a shave, and his skin was burnished from countless seasons in the summer sun. Brushing and flossing had never been a priority for Stumpy, especially now that he was down to only four teeth across the front of his mouth.

Stumpy flashed his picket-fence grin at Barlow, pumping the sheriff's hand and slapping his back as he filled two oversized mugs with steaming black coffee. Barlow thanked him for the java and asked what Stumpy knew about Senator Dunbar and his political connections.

"More than we can cover today," Stumpy said. "What do you want to know?"

"A few years ago, Dunbar was on the front lines of that tort reform stuff in the legislature. Who was in on that with him?"

"There were a lot of them," Stumpy said. "The Republicans had all the seats, and everybody between Texarkana and El Paso wanted to claim credit for getting rid of frivolous lawsuits and keeping down the cost of medical care." Stumpy rolled his eyes. "But the big players were the House speaker, the lieutenant governor, and three or

THE PRICE OF LIFE

four others in the legislature. There was Atkins from Houston, Gonzalez from San Antonio, and Freeman from Dallas, as I recall."

"Any other major players?" Barlow asked.

"No other politicians, but they had some lobbyists and some public relations folks involved. Seemed like they imported some Yankees to do the television stuff, since us Texans are too dumb to do that ourselves," Stumpy replied. "Of course, there were a slew of lawyers, mostly from Washington and New York. I remember one of those guys moved to Austin and spent a hell of a lot of time around Dunbar. Why?"

Barlow's tingle turned into a full-fledged itch.

"Tell me about the lawyer from Austin," he said, ignoring the question.

"He was here at the lake quite a bit with Dunbar," Stumpy said. "Brought his boat, a beauty, and a different young lady every time. Those ladies were prettier than the boat. Anyway, Dunbar would go down to Austin to see this guy, too. Took his boat sometimes, sometimes rode around on the lawyer's boat. They got to be running buddies. I went down to Austin a couple of times to see games at UT with them. Sat in a suite, courtesy of the guy's law firm. Free drinks, free eats, the whole shebang."

"You remember the guy's name?"

Stumpy tilted his head just a bit to the left, thinking hard. "Sellers, something like that," he guessed.

"Bill Sellett?"

"Bingo." Stumpy grinned. "You know him?"

"Never met him." Barlow held up the newspaper for Stumpy to see. "But lots more folks know him today than yesterday."

The headline read: *Austin Attorney William Sellett Slain*.

Stumpy's gap-toothed grin vanished.

# CHAPTER 26

Sheriff Barlow arrived at the FBI's Fort Worth field office a few minutes after nine. He'd called Special Agent Will Thompson, the agent working the Dunbar investigation, and told him he wanted to meet in person to discuss some important developments that might be of interest to him. The FBI man had pressed Barlow to discuss the matter with him on the telephone, but Barlow had insisted on coming to town and said he thought it was crucial to meet in person.

The field office was downtown in a drab, institutional building typical of government construction from the fifties. Barlow showed his credentials to the guards in the lobby and checked his gun before riding up to the fifth floor, where he was greeted by a federal marshal with limited patience and less sense of humor. He waited while the marshal called to verify that Sheriff Barlow was expected. Only then did he allow Barlow to enter his domain, and only with a long, icy stare to clearly state the marshal's sense of superiority.

Special Agent Will Thompson was much more accommodating. He grabbed two navy blue coffee mugs embossed with the agency's unmistakable logo in large gold block letters. "How do you take it?"

"Just black, thanks."

"Good man," Thompson said. "No need to trick it up with milk and sugar, if you ask me."

Barlow nodded and took a sip of the steaming black liquid. He looked around at Thompson's cramped office and noticed a fine oak credenza, out of place behind the standard-issue metal desk and chair. On the credenza sat several framed photos, including one taken at Thompson's graduation from the FBI Academy. A smiling couple, obviously his parents, stood at his side.

On the yellowed wall above, Barlow saw a certificate of appreciation from the Denver Police Department, along with several commendations recognizing Thompson for various achievements as a police officer. Next to the police awards, in a triple-matted frame of unfinished cedar, hung a diploma conferring a Masters degree in criminal justice from Colorado State University. A quick look back at the commendations told Barlow that Will Thompson had earned the degree while working as a patrolman in Denver.

Barlow turned to a side wall and saw the FBI Academy completion certificate placed in the center of a large frame and surrounded by Thompson's FBI certificates for marksmanship, hand-to-hand combat, and threat recognition. A quick glance back at Thompson convinced Barlow that these awards were well-earned. Thompson was the wiry type, with boyish features making him appear much younger than his thirty-three years. He had a hardened, serious look in his dark brown eyes.

Set apart from the main group of FBI certificates was an award for Best of Class on the Yellow Brick Road.

"What's this?" Barlow asked.

"Never heard of the Yellow Brick Road?" asked Thompson.

"Just the one in the movie."

Thompson sipped his coffee. "The Yellow Brick Road is a series of running and obstacle courses for FBI trainees. It starts with a two-miler called Not in Kansas Anymore. Then came the Tin Man Trot, the Gates of Oz, and the Munchkin Trail. You get the idea."

Barlow nodded over the rim of his mug.

"All of these runs lead to the Yellow Brick Road," Thompson continued, leaning back in his chair. "The Academy started a Fitness Challenge in 1981, and they give bricks to the cadets who finished. The trainees started painting their bricks yellow and placing them along the path at the end of the last run. There are now about fourteen thousand yellow bricks on that path."

"And you were the best in your class?" asked Barlow, clearly impressed.

"Actually, it's a competition with four-man teams. The run covers six miles. We scale walls with ropes, climb over cargo nets, and dive through window openings. Right near the finish, after climbing one of the six walls on the course, we crawl on our bellies through mud for about seventy-five yards under razor wire, then run the last quarter mile to the finish. Our team set the course record."

"Outstanding," chimed Barlow. "Still like to run?"

"I try to do five or six miles every day. I like the Trinity Trail early in the morning." Thompson set down his mug. "So, sheriff, what can I help you with today?"

"I wanted to tell you a little about the Ken Dunbar case. I think there may be a connected case down in Austin."

Thompson's square jaw clenched. "You have my attention."

"You ever hear of Bill Sellett, a lawyer from Austin?" Barlow asked.

"I saw the article in yesterday's paper about him. He got killed a few days ago at his house in Austin."

Barlow paused. "I think his case might be connected to the Dunbar murder."

"I'm listening."

"Nothing about the cases jumped out. Dunbar was killed on the highway, and Sellett at his house. The crime scenes are about a hundred fifty miles apart. Murder weapon in the Dunbar case was a knife, but never recovered. Ditto with Sellett, although he was attacked with a club of some kind, also not recovered.

"Then I read the article in the *Star Telegram*, which said that Sellett was a lobbyist involved in tort reform legislation."

"I saw that, too, but that was before my time," Thompson said. "I spent my first two years in Miami before I got transferred here."

"Lucky man," Barlow said. "You know what folks say. I wasn't born in Texas--"

"--but I got here as fast as I could," Thompson interrupted, momentarily lightening the mood.

"Absolutely. Anyhow, Dunbar was on the legislative committee that drafted the tort reform package, and he was a vocal supporter."

"So the senator and the lobbyist worked on the same bills a few years ago, so what?" Thompson seemed to lose interest. "Do we list all of the opponents of the bill as suspects?"

"No, sir," Barlow replied, "and if that was all of it, I wouldn't be here. I checked with a few people, and it turns out Dunbar and Sellett were close, and stayed close after the law passed. They hung out together at the lake out our way, and down in the Hill Country. They went to football games together in Austin. And Sellett was supposed to visit at Dunbar's lake house the week after Dunbar's murder."

"Who told you all this?" Thompson asked, suddenly interested again.

"A few folks," Barlow said. "Stumpy LeGrande, for one."

"The old drunk at Possum Kingdom?"

"He's not a drunk. He just likes to drink," Barlow said with a shrug. "And you might change your tune if you knew he liked to drink with Dunbar and Sellett. At Possum Kingdom, at Lake Travis, at football games. He was part of the group. I talked to Dunbar's widow. She confirmed they'd become close friends."

"This is fascinating," said Thompson, "but how do we connect the victims to the same perpetrator?"

"Well, sir, that's why I'm talking to Special Agent Will Thompson of the Federal Bureau of Investigation."

For the next two hours, Thompson took Barlow through the maze of administration to get the necessary authorizations to expand the investigation and treat the cases as connected. They obtained approval from Washington for Barlow to participate and share evidence collected and catalogued by the FBI, although permission for Barlow's deputy to do the same was denied. Finally, Thompson received approval from his boss in Fort Worth to access the full resources of the Bureau, including lab techs, computers, and other agents, without additional approval each time he needed it. It was a productive two hours.

Afterward, over burgers and onion rings at Kincaid's, Thompson asked how Barlow had gotten into law enforcement.

Barlow shrugged. "I backed in, I guess. I was born and raised in Mineral Wells and came back home after college and a couple years in the service."

"Military Police?" Thompson asked around a bite of cheeseburger.

"Yep. Got a job as a cop, then ran for sheriff on a whim. I was twenty-eight, the youngest sheriff ever elected. I guess it came in handy that I played on the state finalist football team two years in a row."

"Sounds like you like your gig."

"You could say that," Barlow agreed. "Never was much of a city boy. Could've gone to UT, but got a ranch management degree from Tarleton instead. Now I'm full-time sheriff and part-time cattle rancher, and I figure that'll do as long as the folks in Palo Pinto want me to work for them."

Barlow wiped his hands with a paper towel and asked about the plans for their investigation. Thompson spent a few minutes running down the list of things to do, including a thorough review of the evidence collected from each crime scene and cross checking each set against the other. They would look for anything in common, anything that might point them in the direction of a single killer.

"So, Kimo Sabe, where do we start?" asked Barlow.

Thompson wiped his mouth after polishing off the last of his onion rings. "Well, Tonto, are you up for a road trip to Austin?"

# CHAPTER 27

After his successful trip to Seattle, Grant returned to San Antonio for the deposition of Dr. Richard Perkins. If the Howard deposition was a victory, the Perkins depo was a blowout. T. Scott Wynn had received medical records on the last twelve cases done by Dr. Perkins, which confirmed Dr. Howard's testimony about the success of the laser procedure in treating the kind of brain tumor that killed Jennifer Haller.

Wynn was decidedly less enthusiastic than he'd been at the beginning of the Howard deposition, especially when he discovered that he couldn't harass Dr. Perkins about his fees. Part of the reason for Wynn's subdued disposition, Grant thought, must have been the menacing presence of Ed Haller, who glowered across the table for the duration of the proceedings. Grant had noticed how Haller's presence had thrown Wynn off track during the first round of depositions and was delighted when Haller expressed an interest in hearing Perkins testify.

Whatever the reason, Wynn took scarcely more than two hours with Perkins, seemingly satisfied to ask for a list of opinions and have Perkins tell him about the last twelve cases. The summary was that each and every patient had survived with absolutely no adverse effects. When the deposition was over, the case had progressed to a point that even Grant hadn't expected. Haller sensed this as well, which wasn't necessarily a good thing.

"So now they talk to us about settlement, right?" Haller asked as they walked out of the conference room.

"Probably not." Grant shook his head.

"I don't understand," Haller argued. "Dr. Perkins just told them he could have saved Jennifer's life, and she'd be fine if Purser had just ordered the CT scan. Wynn didn't even put up a fight."

"This wasn't the place for them to fight," said Grant. "They have experts, too, and good ones. Their counterpart to Dr. Perkins is a surgeon in New York named Samuel Fletcher. Fletcher was Perkins' mentor in a fellowship program fifteen years ago. He's the only doctor in the country with more experience treating these tumors than Perkins. I go to New York in a couple of weeks to take his deposition, and it'll probably look a lot like today, but in reverse."

Grant stopped. He turned to Haller and sighed heavily. "Their neurologist is the chief of the department at Dallas Memorial and the head professor of neurology at the UT Medical Center. These people are serious, and they're pulling out all the stops."

"I don't get it," said Haller. "I thought they'd look at the guys on our team and figure they ought to cough up their money early instead of spending it defending a case they shouldn't win."

Grant took another deep breath. He'd already covered this and his frustration was mounting. "Captain Haller, please remember what we talked about when you hired me. Especially in malpractice cases, insurance companies don't think of the money they pay to their attorneys in the same way they think of money they pay to plaintiffs. They don't even blink when doctors charge them a thousand bucks an hour for doing expert work. They fight with their lawyers about rates and about every minute billed, but they do that more for amusement. They're not worried about attorney's fees.

"Paying settlements is entirely different. The money comes out of different accounts, for one thing. With the recovery limited to $250,000, why should they worry about settling cases?

"If they go to trial and win, the money they spent on lawyers and experts was well worth it. If they lose, they cut a check for two-fifty and move on. They only to settle a case if they might have to pay huge damages for killing somebody who made a lot of money. They worry about those cases and they settle them. Others, like yours, they roll the dice and take their chances."

"That's the price of my daughter's life?" Haller seethed. "And not even that until we win?" Haller's jaw was tightly clenched and a vein in his temple pulsed visibly.

"No, Ed," Grant said. "Jennifer's life was priceless. So was she. But we'll do all we can to make them pay as much as we can in this lawsuit."

"And that's supposed to be okay? I'm supposed to think that makes everything right?" Haller's pain was palpable, his eyes flashing and his face hardening into a mask of rage. Grant's soothing tone hadn't accomplished its goal.

"No, Ed, it's not okay." Grant tried again, grasping his client's shoulder firmly. "This is what we've talked about. It's not the value of your daughter. It never could be. It's the value of the case that arose because she died. All we can do is the best job possible to get the most money for that case. That's it. I know it's not enough. But it's all we have."

They exchanged a long look before Haller spoke. "You have kids, Mr. Mercer?"

"Two girls."

"If one of them died like Jennifer did, you think you'd be okay with two-fifty?"

Grant didn't hesitate. "No, I wouldn't."

Haller's expression softened ever so slightly. "Thank you for your hard work, Mr. Mercer," he said. "I know you're doing your best."

The two men shook hands as they parted, and Grant watched Haller disappear around the corner of the parking garage. As he walked slowly to his truck, he wondered whether he had handled Haller's last question as well as he should have. It was the truth, but it was hardly reassuring to a client struggling to fight through the most agonizing time of his life.

All the way home to Fort Worth, Grant gnawed on the case in his head, re-running the depositions already done and making a series of mental notes for those still to be taken. As he approached Fort Worth, Chris Turner called. Although they spoke on the phone regularly, he and Turner had seen each other infrequently since the trial of the Middleton case, and Grant was happy to hear from him.

"Come get a beer with me tonight," said Chris. "The wife and kids are with the in-laws tonight and I got a kitchen pass. Let's go to the Flying Saucer and watch the game."

Grant had lost all track of things outside the case and asked his friend what sport he was talking about.

"Mavs, dumbass." Turner chuckled. "Season opener against the Spurs."

Grant had listened to the sports talk shows in San Antonio discussing how the Spurs would avenge their loss to Dallas in last year's playoffs by beating the Mavericks to start off the new season. "Sounds good. What time is the game?"

"Tip-off is at seven, but I planned on leaving in a few minutes and getting us a good table."

"Sure thing," said Grant. "I'm about twenty minutes from downtown. See you at the Saucer."

# CHAPTER 28

True to his word, Chris Turner arrived early and secured a primo table at the Flying Saucer beer emporium in Sundance Square. The Saucer had been there almost twenty years and provided a front row seat to the transformation of downtown Fort Worth. Years ago, the central business district started a slow downward spiral as businesses, shops, restaurants and movie theatres moved to the suburbs. The area became a darkened ghost town after six in the evening.

In the early eighties, a couple of brothers who'd enjoyed tremendous success in the oil business in Fort Worth took it upon themselves to reverse the trend. They bought buildings by the dozen and began the push with the city to repair streets, add lighting, and commit to a police presence in the evenings. They and the city offered incentives for restaurants, retail, and other businesses to come downtown and converted several of the old buildings to condos and apartments to draw residents to the city center.

Soon, Fort Worth sported the best downtown in the state, perhaps in the entire southwest. Cops on horseback patrolled well-lit streets and sidewalks. People flocked to the area to see movies, enjoy dinner and drinks, and take in live music. In the early nineties, work was completed on the Bass Performance Hall, the last great opera house built in the twentieth century. Directly across the street stood the Flying Saucer, where a rowdy Thursday night crowd would sample ales and lagers from around the globe while cheering on the Dallas Mavericks.

Grant arrived at six-thirty and pulled his chair into the table across the corner from Chris after the two shook hands and embraced.

"You look like crap," Chris said, his usual greeting.

"And you look like week old crap," came the standard reply from Grant. "Black and tans on the way?"

"Just what the doctor ordered," said Chris. "So how's it going?"

"Great. Never better."

"Me, too."

A short pause followed. It had become ritual for these two friends to have the typical guy exchange at the beginning of each meeting. Part of it was because neither wanted to wander too far, at least right away, from the usual rules of guy conversation, which dictate that there shall be no discussion of feelings, sports must be addressed at least once in each meeting, and no weakness shall be revealed by an admission that things in a guy's life are going anything but great.

The problem is that men do, in fact, have feelings, sports don't always rise to the top of their priority list, and sometimes, no matter how fortunate they are, their lives are not great. Good friends don't just participate in the opening ritual, they push through it to the truth beyond. They understand the desire to put up the defense and the need for a sympathetic ear to listen when life's reality disrupts our grandiose plans with its customary brutality. Men need good friends for times like these, and too often don't have them.

Above all, men need good friends because a man needs somebody who can tell him he's full of shit when he starts spouting off half-cocked ideas. Wives often fill that role, as do bosses, business rivals, and children, but a good friend can do it and still be a good friend. More to the point, a man might believe the good friend and take a good look inward. He might decide the friend is right, he is full of shit. It's complicated, but absolutely necessary in every man's life.

In Chris Turner, Grant had found a good friend who understood all of these things. Grant had actually been there for Chris first, when his father went through the final stages of Parkinson's disease. Chris tried to balance a busy law practice, a young family, and the constant need to assist his mother with the daily ordeal of caring for a man who could no longer care for himself. Each of these things took its separate toll, and when added to the emotional strain of watching his father deteriorate, it was too much for Chris to handle.

One day about a week before his father died, all of it came tumbling down. Chris started his drive to work, but when he got within a few blocks of the office he found he simply couldn't drive any farther. He couldn't return home. His wife would notice his distress, and her dismissal of his emotional condition would only make matters worse. He called Grant instead. Over several cups of Starbucks House Blend, Grant listened to his friend, hearing the despair in Chris' voice.

Grant let Chris know that others had survived the same journey, and the knowledge that he wasn't alone was a lifeline to Chris. Thanks in large part to Grant's sympathetic ear, Chris had managed to salvage his career and save his marriage, and he'd repaid Grant in kind through the years. Tonight was another installment.

Halfway through his second beer, Grant spoke up. "Man, this case might just finish me off."

"What's happening now?" Chris asked. "Last I heard, it sounded like things were going so well."

"In a way, they are," Grant admitted. "Scott Wynn just took my two experts' depositions, and they went great. In fact, I was in San

Antonio today for Richard Perkins' depo, and Wynn barely laid a glove on him. He pretty much mailed it in."

"You taking his guys soon?"

"New York next month to depose Fletcher at Bellevue, then their neuro, Rucker, over at UT Southwestern."

Chris flinched. "Last time I deposed him, Rucker took me to the woodshed. And isn't Fletcher the guy in New York who was Perkins' mentor in the neurosurgery fellowship?"

"You're catching on," Grant said, pulling on the dark upper layer of the black and tan. "Still, that's not what has me bugged. I'm ready for the depos, and they can't argue with Perkins' success in his program, whether Fletcher taught him fifteen years ago or not." Grant took a moment to give Chris a brief explanation of Perkins' study program in San Antonio and his perfect success rate in the last dozen procedures.

Chris waved at the waitress and signaled for another round. "Why don't you tell me what's bugging you?"

"It's the reason everybody got out of the med mal game, Chris. Nobody can get happy with a case like this. My clients are a couple of fantastic people. He's a Marine with a purple heart after four tours in Iraq. He lost his leg, but he's training for a marathon in six months. He wants to qualify for Boston, and he'll probably do it. His wife's a gem, best client you could ever want.

"But they're just like anyone else. They don't understand how there can be a limit on recovery for the death of their daughter. We had the same discussion I have with all my clients. I told them about the cap and answered all the usual questions about whether there was any way to get more. I know they understand, because they're smart people. But they're having a hard time getting their minds wrapped around it."

"That's the case with every client these days, isn't it?" asked Chris.

"Yeah, it is," agreed Grant. "My partner's driving me nuts about it, too. He wants to know why we want a case where the maximum fee is a $100,000, and we have to give twenty-five percent to you for the referral. If it wasn't for Perkins doing the expert work for free, we'd have fifty grand in it by now. As it is, we have about thirty, and more to spend."

"You knew all this when you got into it, right?" asked Turner.

Grant nodded.

"Then what's the problem?"

"The problem is this. I took this case in spite of the fact that I knew it wouldn't bring a big fee. I took it knowing full well my clients' share of the recovery would be less than the fees and expenses it'll take to get the recovery, and we get paid only if we win at trial. Neither my client nor my partner will be satisfied with the best result I can get for them, and there's nothing I can do about it. I'm starting to wonder whether it might be best to cut our losses, see if they'll just pay us one-fifty or so, reduce the fees, and get it over with. Do you know how hard a trial will be on the Hallers?"

Chris leaned forward. "Is this about them, or is it about you?"

"What the hell does that mean?"

"It means this," said Chris, looking Grant straight in the eye. "You took the case because you thought it was the right thing to do, and it looks like you're starting to wonder whether you made the right decision."

"Right, but I just told you that." Grant's irritation was growing steadily.

"You made the right decision, Grant, and you made it for the right reasons. Sometimes we do things for reasons other than money.

133

In fact, we're supposed to do the right thing and hope the money follows. A friend of mine once said that's why they call it a profession and not a business."

Grant knew he was being quoted, but said nothing.

"You remember old man Collins holding court in the break room on Saturday mornings?"

"Not really." Grant shook his head. "I was never a big fan of Saturday morning face time."

"Well, I was there every Saturday, even after you left," Chris said. "One morning Collins was talking about the lawyer who was trying the case against him at the time. Watching those two go at it in trial, you'd have thought Collins hated the guy. But there he sat singing his opponent's praises. You and I both thought he was just blowing smoke, so that if Collins lost it would look like he got beat by a great lawyer."

Grant nodded and sipped his beer.

"He said something that day I'll never forget. He said he respected the guy because he believed in his case. The lawyer knew he was up against long odds. But he made a commitment to his client and was seeing the commitment through. Not because he might make a big fee if he won, but because it was the right thing to do. There were a lot of things about old man Collins I didn't like, but that day I found one thing I've always liked. He knew about integrity, and he recognized it in the people around him."

"True," said Grant, "but that doesn't help me, does it?"

"That depends how well you paid attention to Collins and what he was trying to teach us." Chris took a swig of Guinness, wiped the creamy foam from his lip with the back of his hand, and leaned in again. "It also depends on whether you're willing to quit feeling sorry for yourself and get on with your case."

Chris watched as Grant's expression turned from self-pity to anger to embarrassment in the space of about five seconds.

"When you took the case, you promised the Hallers you'd do your best for them. You explained everything they needed to know, so they could decide for themselves whether they wanted to get into this case and expose themselves to the emotional turmoil that comes along with it.

"You told your partner all about the case, including the limit on damages. He might not have been wild about it, but he left the decision to you. And even though it won't be as much as it should be, the fee from a maximum recovery will work out better than the hourly rate you'd get from one of the firm's insurance clients. What I'm saying is everybody here is a grownup, capable of making decisions. Those decisions were made. The only thing to do now is finish the job."

"You're right," Grant said. "The only people I should worry about at this point are Ed and Julie Haller. They put their trust in me to get justice for the death of their little girl. If I don't do that, who will?"

"Good question," Chris said before finishing off his black and tan. "Who will?"

# CHAPTER 29

Grant walked into his house at ten-fifteen. The whole place was dark. He flipped on the light in the living room and turned it off again when he got to the other side of the room. As he approached the master bedroom door, he noticed it was open just a crack and saw faint light peeking around the edge. He heard the soft strains of Sarah McLachlan as he eased the door open to find Samantha lying across the bed, head propped in one hand and a glass of white wine in the other.

Candles glowed from a half dozen places around the room, their light bouncing off the faux stone finish of the walls and shimmering in her hair as it flowed around her neck and shoulders. She wore a black negligee, which barely covered her full breasts with scalloped lace and was scarcely long enough to hide the sheer black thong encircling her hips.

"Hello, there," she cooed. "Had a long day?"

"Can't complain. My wife gave me a pass to have a couple of beers and watch basketball with a buddy. Pretty good day, actually."

"Then how about a bath, a glass of wine, and me?" Samantha asked playfully, running her finger along the rim of her wine glass.

"Sure." Grant smiled. "Looks like you've already been in the tub."

"I have. Now get your cute ass in there and get cleaned up."

As he slid into the hot water, Samantha appeared with a glass of wine in each hand, handing one to him with a mischievous grin. She sat on the edge of the tub, then leaned over and kissed him, lingering a few extra seconds to enjoy the taste of the wine from his lips.

"How did it go in San Antonio?" she asked.

"Perkins is a pro. He handled Scott Wynn like I knew he would."

"You said something about Ed Haller when you called. Everything okay?"

Grant took another sip of the chilled wine and slid lower into the water. "It's the same as I see with all these clients. He's a smart guy, and he hears the words. He just can't see how it's a good thing that his daughter is dead and there's a limit on what the man responsible will have to pay."

"Didn't you have the usual talk with him?" Samantha asked, rubbing a soapy washcloth across his chest.

"Sure did," Grant said. "But when I talk to him, I can tell he's in pain. He doesn't show much, but he hurts. Maybe more than any other client I've ever had. I think it might be worse for him because he was overseas, then came back missing a leg. The whole time his daughter was going through treatment for her tumor, he was recovering, too. He never had a chance to comfort her, just to be with her. I think it's killing him inside."

"What are you going to do?"

"All I can do," said Grant. "I'll do the best I can to get them the two-fifty. What else can I do?"

"You do what you can," Samantha said. "I'm proud of you, and I'm sure Ed and Julie appreciate what you're doing for them."

They were both quiet for a long moment before Samantha spoke. "You sure you're okay?"

"Absolutely."

"Then maybe you can do something I can appreciate," purred Samantha, leaning over to kiss him again.

As she gently brushed his lips and tongue with the tip of hers, Samantha's hand slipped into the water and below Grant's waist. After a moment, Grant stood, Samantha wrapping a towel around his shoulders.

"Don't be long," she said, stepping through the door into the bedroom.

Grant dried off quickly and moved to the bed. He leaned over his wife, kissing her deeply. He moved his hand across her belly, sliding the silk fabric of the negligee up and aside to feel the softness of her skin. His touch brought out a tiny gasp and tightened her flesh from her neck to her knees. Grant then hooked a thumb between her abdomen and the soft lace waistband of her thong and slid the thumb downward, forcing another quick and shallow breath.

As they made love, Grant felt his tension evaporate. He was amazed that after so many years it still felt so much like new. The world shrank until there was nothing except the two of them and the pleasure they gave one another. The physical satisfaction was important to Grant, but the simple fact was that he loved her beyond all reason and craved the intimacy of their souls that only the union of their bodies could bring. There were cards, notes, and conversation, and Grant never had trouble telling Samantha how much he loved her. Still, for him, the desire to be one with her was so strong that nothing else reached the part of his heart craving that fulfillment.

Afterward, cradling his sleeping wife's head against his shoulder, Grant's thoughts again turned to Ed and Julie Haller. He'd handled many cases involving the death of loved ones. It was easy to become jaded about such things, to think only in terms of cases, issues, and settlement value. Grant had resisted the temptation, perhaps to the detriment of his career.

He honestly didn't know how parents coped with the death of a child and believed he would simply collapse, unable to deal with the pain, if his son or daughter were taken from him. He wasn't a man with many fears, but the thought of his children dying broke him out in a cold sweat. If he thought someone else was responsible for the death of his child, he would make it his mission to extract a terrible price.

Grant understood what Haller had said, that he considered it his sworn duty to stand up for his daughter and seek justice for her death.

At least I'm not a sword or a gun, he thought. At least we've evolved to the point that we seek justice in a civilized manner rather than dueling at dawn. Even if it's not the perfect career, Grant thought, the law serves the noble purpose of keeping us from resorting to violence when we're wronged. Grant never considered himself a weapon of vengeance, but he now realized that's exactly what he was. A civilized weapon, perhaps, but a weapon just the same.

With these thoughts to comfort him, Grant drifted off to sleep.

# CHAPTER 30

Crisp evening air greeted Grant when he stepped out of the terminal at LaGuardia Airport. Grant especially loved to visit New York when autumn came. Eighty-five degrees when he had boarded the plane at D/FW had become a refreshing forty-eight at sunset in Queens.

The flight had been uneventful, and Grant had been upgraded to first class at the last minute. It was one of the few benefits to flying more than a million miles in a two-year stretch. From his window seat on the left side of the plane he had a perfect view of the Manhattan skyline as they landed, the seemingly endless rows of skyscrapers fronted by the East River and backlit by the sun finishing its journey toward the Pacific.

Grant had come to love New York after a childhood being conditioned to hate it. Grant's father, like most Texans of the time, considered New York an immoral and filthy place where only multimillionaires could live above the poverty line. Samantha was a Texas girl born and bred, her fear and loathing of New York ingrained in a similar fashion. For several years, Grant would suggest a visit to Gotham for a long weekend, where they could take in a show or two, walk in Central Park, and window shop on Fifth Avenue. She refused every time. Finally, he arranged a trip to New York for a deposition and convinced Samantha to come along. She loved it.

Samantha was utterly mesmerized by the Broadway performances, and the city captured her heart and her imagination with its constant, irrepressible pulse. They now returned every couple of years to buy fake Rolexes and handbags on Canal Street, visit museums, and see a show.

The deposition of Dr. Samuel Fletcher would take place in the middle of the week, and Samantha had to be home for the never-ending school events during the month or two before Christmas. Grant would not, however, be alone for the entire trip. Ed Haller had clearly enjoyed the experience of being face-to-face with T. Scott Wynn in Dr. Perkins' deposition and wanted to eyeball the defendant's expert witnesses, too. He told Grant he had to be in Washington for a military conference during the same week and would come to New York for the deposition. Grant gave Haller the schedule and location and arranged to meet him at the conference room a half hour early.

Grant took a cab into the city and arrived at his hotel a little before seven. The Exchange Hotel was in lower Manhattan, a block from the Seaport and three blocks from the New York Stock Exchange. He preferred the Hotel on Rivington, a new Tribeca high rise with floor-to-ceiling glass walls and a perfect location for shopping and dining, but the Exchange was just a five-minute cab ride from Bellevue Hospital, where the deposition would take place. It would do just fine for his purposes on this trip.

After checking in, he took about an hour to review his outline of questions for Dr. Fletcher and a few of the key medical records. With that accomplished, he left the hotel and rode the subway to the stop at Broadway and Houston. Four blocks later he entered The Spice Market, where he ate seared ahi tuna on a bed of sobe noodles, paired with a lovely Pinot Noir from the Russian River Valley. The waiter tried to talk him into a Burgundy for a dollar less per glass, but Grant had developed a preference for California wines over those from France. He felt sure the waiter chalked him up as another guy from west of the Hudson who didn't know diddly about wine. Regardless, Grant enjoyed the Pinot and ordered a second glass, just to watch the waiter's reaction.

As he savored the currant and tobacco hints in the rich bouquet of the wine, he looked casually around the restaurant and remembered his visit for dinner with his daughter on her first trip to New York. She had just turned eighteen and was about to begin her senior year in high school. Grant had planned the trip as a surprise, picking her up for lunch one day and taking her straight to the airport with the suitcase her mother had packed.

Grant and Angela saw four shows in three days. They spent afternoons in parks and museums and ate late dinners, talking into the wee hours about Angela's career plans, college choices, and her interest in music, foreign language, and travel. The weekend was absolutely magical, and it instilled in his daughter a love for New York.

Grant would always remember how she cherished their trip, taken at such a pivotal time in her life. He'd watched his little girl become a woman before his very eyes, and he loved the fact that for the rest of her life, whenever Angela visited or so much as thought of New York, she would know it was her father who'd made the introduction.

Nourished and relaxed, Grant returned to the hotel and called Samantha to hear about the night's choir performance. He was asleep by ten and would be rested and ready for the impending skirmish with Samuel Fletcher, MD.

# CHAPTER 31

Perched high above the hustle of Lower Manhattan, Lewis Cashman surveyed his domain. From his steel and glass desk, he scanned from the Brooklyn Bridge to the Statue of Liberty, then up the west side of the island to Midtown. It was an office befitting the Chief Executive Officer of a world-wide insurance company, and he loved all one 1,320 square feet of it. He casually strolled toward the conversation area, with its burgundy leather sofa and chairs, plopping his rotund derriere down into the center of the sofa and leaning back to take a long swallow of cold Canadian glacier water.

Every week, another two cases were delivered to his office suite, along with the paperwork certifying its collection from the melt of a glacier in British Columbia. The stuff cost eight dollars a bottle including shipping, and was the only water Cashman would drink.

From across the room, he admired the ten-foot mahogany conference table surrounded by eight chairs and topped with a Remington bronze of a horse and rider stomping a snake. The bar in one corner allowed him convenient access to his beloved Woodford Reserve small-batch bourbon, which he enjoyed almost as much as the office itself.

Cashman poured himself a double Woodford, no ice, to go with the glacier water, and took in about half of it in one long pull.

Savoring the musky taste and the gentle burn down his gullet, he walked behind the bar, through a beautiful carved wooden door, and into the executive suite provided by Castle Guard Insurance Company for its Chief Executive.

He stepped into the private bathroom and splashed cool water on his face. The reflection looking back at him wasn't a particularly pleasant sight. Cashman's hair, once dark, full, and wavy, now barely covered his white, shiny scalp. Sallow skin hung from his neck, jowls folding over the top of the collar of his pricey white cotton dress shirt. Deep, dark bags lay under each of his dull and beady eyes, which seemed to sink farther into his skull with each passing week.

Drying off with the Egyptian cotton hand towel, he admired the rest of the space. Travertine tile of varying shades lined a steam shower equipped with spray nozzles capable of reaching every crevice with piping hot water. Ostensibly a place to stay after working late hours at the office, the executive suite had been a veritable bachelor pad for Cashman. With his wife spending the majority of her time at their Westchester home, it became Cashman's habit to spend three or four nights each week in the city.

His wife had become old before her time. She'd fallen miserably out of shape, progressing from a size six on their wedding day through size ten, then twelve, and ultimately to her current size sixteen. No measure of gentle prodding, and none of his more direct attacks on her appearance, motivated her to get out of the boutiques of Fifth Avenue and into a gym.

The irony of such conversations was entirely lost on Cashman, whose own appearance had regressed from unattractive at twenty-five to downright slovenly at fifty-eight. He'd gained nearly sixty pounds in thirty years and had devoted almost no effort to stopping the slide. He hadn't graced the inside of a gym in more than ten years, and seriously doubted he could run a hundred yards without inviting a heart attack.

Cashman's wife had also lost all interest in sex, preferring shopping as her favorite pastime. This was something Cashman hadn't minded, and figured his astronomical credit card bills were a fair price for the distraction of his wife from his frequent dalliances.

Cashman lived in the city during the week while his wife stayed home on Long Island, but he never lacked for companionship. Beautiful women from twenty-five to forty-five provided constant arm charms at the finest restaurants in town, shows in the theatre district, and receptions for various charitable organizations. Cashman had been approached by several women in their fifties, but promptly rejected the notion of a fling with a woman in his own demographic category.

To many, it appeared that Cashman was single. To those who knew he was married, the simple explanation was that the women were underlings at the company or clients who needed attention, or perhaps escorts hired to give the president of the company the shine he needed. To Cashman, it was simply his right to have the company and sexual energy of young and beautiful ladies.

Cashman peered across the Hudson River at the twinkling lights of New Jersey and smiled to himself. Another great day in the books, and a great evening was about to unfold. He was heading out for dinner with one of the current stable of lovelies, Rebecca McDermott. Rebecca was thirty-six, petite, and predictably stunning. Her smile was suited to toothpaste commercials, and her high cheekbones could have landed her on the cover of half a dozen magazines.

To her credit, she hadn't relied exclusively on her looks in college, and had earned a Masters degree in Finance to go along with her bachelor's degree in Management. These days, she was an Assistant Vice President of Castle Guard, with an office in Mid-town, a six-figure income, and a bright future with the company. She'd hitched her wagon to Lewis Cashman and was now cementing the professional relationship with something a bit more personal.

Cashman had been pleased to discover that she was as energetic in the bedroom as she was in the board room, although a bit distressed that he often found it impossible to keep up. He occasionally found himself considering an exclusive arrangement with Rebecca, but the thought of a committed sexual relationship with only one gorgeous girl at a time was a bit depressing, and he'd easily set aside such a ridiculous idea.

Freshened as well as possible, Cashman re-entered the business portion of the floor, grabbed his briefcase, and headed to the door. He bid a perfunctory good night to his assistants and secretary on the way to the elevator, reminding them that tomorrow would be another busy day. This merry band of flunkies would work long into the night to ensure that their boss was seen in the best possible light, but this thought no longer registered in Cashman's conscious mind. In fact, the only time he thought about his staff was when one of the group was missing.

It was a pleasant evening, and Cashman decided to walk a few blocks, maybe stop for a quick drink before meeting Rebecca for dinner. He pushed through the revolving door in the lobby, turned right onto Water Street, then left on William Street before heading in the direction of the New York Stock Exchange. His head and shoulders bobbed along as he joined the heavy pedestrian traffic filling the sidewalk.

Cashman entered the door of a bar halfway down the block and soon had an icy Stolichnaya martini in hand. As he drank the first half of the slushy vodka, he felt the impact on his stomach, the spread of the warmth through his belly and up into his chest, and the familiar tingle on his scalp. The involuntary shiver finished off the run of sensory delights from the first swallow of the martini. Cashman wished he could stay for two, but Rebecca McDermott and her megawatt smile were waiting.

# CHAPTER 32

Rebecca McDermott, for all her education and professional accomplishments, still subscribed to *People* magazine and was an unabashed celebrity watcher. This explained their presence at Tribeca Grill, where star sightings were commonplace. "Isn't that Brad Pitt?" she asked.

"I don't see Angie or any of the two dozen kids, so I doubt it." Cashman scowled. "Is that really the only reason you wanted to come here?"

"The food's great, too, don't you think?"

Cashman looked down at his seared sea scallops with chanterelles and corn pudding. "Mine is fabulous, but what are you doing with the poor man's *osso bucco*?"

"They're short ribs," Rebecca corrected, "and they're wonderful. The little porcini mushrooms are delectable."

Cashman felt the gnawing ache of desire as he watched Rebecca delicately slip a forkful of beef into her mouth. "Pumpkin crème brulee with espresso?"

"Mmmmm. Perfect."

After leaving the appropriate amount of her dinner uneaten, Rebecca leaned toward Cashman. "Good appearance for us this evening, I'd say."

"I'm glad you think so," Cashman said. "An event like that draws a lot of press coverage. It's essential for Castle Guard to be regarded as an altruistic and generous corporate citizen. That's why I've created a plan to double our charitable commitments in the next five years."

"Double?" Rebecca's eyebrows arched. "Is the Board going to approve of that kind of charitable spending?"

"No problem," Cashman said as the waiter delivered the custard and coffee. "For each of the five largest charities, I promised our support in exchange for their pledge to convert their insurance coverage to Castle Guard as soon as possible. That should more than pay for our charitable contributions."

"You're a genius, Lewis."

"You're damn right I am." Cashman allowed himself a modest smile. "And don't you forget it."

The happy couple left the restaurant by ten-thirty and hopped into a cab. Although the ride was only a matter of minutes, they couldn't keep their hands off one another. After a short walk from the taxi, the groping continued in the elevator on the way to the executive suite, and Rebecca was barely clad by the time Cashman closed the door behind them.

As usual, he'd prepared for the upcoming evening with a delivery of fresh flowers and had been sure to put a disc into the CD player on the bedside table. The push of a button brought forth Norah Jones breathlessly cooing *Don't Know Why I Didn't Come*. Cashman hoped this wouldn't be the thought on Rebecca's mind once their encounter was complete.

The lighting was adjusted with the slide of the dimmer switch near the headboard, although not so low that Cashman couldn't appreciate the breathtaking sight of Rebecca as she slowly disrobed. As her ridiculously tiny panties hit the floor, she moved toward him with feline grace, never taking her eyes from his. His eyes, of course,

GREG McCARTHY

only strayed to hers occasionally, preferring to take in the flatness of her belly, the swell of her breasts, the athletic strength of her legs, and the glow of her perfectly smooth skin.

He moved for her, but she kept him at bay with one arm, moving her right hand to the knot of his tie and removing it in one motion. She unbuttoned his shirt and opened the front to reveal the expanse of his white V-neck T shirt. She ran her hand across his soft and unimpressive chest, then down across the protruding paunch of his gut, unfastening his belt and reaching for his zipper.

"Come on, baby, I'm ready," she begged.

"I'm trying," Cashman responded. "Sometimes it takes awhile." Sometimes a lot longer with six drinks on board, he thought.

After much too long, Cashman was able to overcome the effects of the alcohol. For the next three minutes, he was again amazed at her energy and passion in bed. Clearly disappointed by the brevity of their first turn, Rebecca allowed only a ten-minute recovery period before demanding further enjoyment. Unable to respond, Cashman rolled over, facing away from her, desperate for sleep. She snuggled against his back, nuzzled his neck, and reached around his waist.

"Let me sleep," he pleaded. "Haven't you had enough?"

"I never have enough of you," she whispered. "You know that."

"Well, I have. I need some sleep. Maybe in the morning?"

She pouted as she turned away.

He followed her, tucking her under his arm, marveling again at her body, the smooth, silky feel of her skin, how she was soft and firm and sleek, all in just the right places. Entirely spent, Cashman finally closed his eyes. He truly wished he could summon the energy to please Rebecca once more. He promised himself, for the third time this month, that he would slow down on the drinking and try to get to the gym at least once a week.

Considering his inadequacies with his concubine, it hadn't been the perfect day. All in all, though, Cashman figured it had been a pretty decent way to spend the evening. There would be plenty of time to make it up to Rebecca.

# CHAPTER 33

Grant's attention sometimes wandered. He often found that one thought would trigger another, and the new thought yet another, until he realized he couldn't even recall what he'd been thinking about in the first place. But when he was in a deposition, his focus was razor-sharp. His cell phone was off, he was out of the office, and multitasking was a distant memory.

Grant often wished he could live his life as if in a deposition, without the distractions of the typical day. It frustrated him to begin work on a project only to have the first of a dozen or more of his staff and associates walk in to ask questions. He'd always been an open-door kind of boss, which endeared him to employees but limited his ability to be productive in the office. If the employees left him alone, the phone would ring and a client, child, or wife would have problems that couldn't possibly be solved without his input.     But     in depositions, it was expected that cell phones and BlackBerries would be turned off and nothing else would be accomplished for the next four to six hours except the pursuit of justice by way of sworn testimony. Grant loved it.

Dr. Samuel Fletcher didn't share Grant's enthusiasm for the process. He was accustomed to people bowing and scraping before him, following his instructions without hesitation, and generally regarding him with fear and awe. Grant displayed none of these traits, and it irritated the doctor to no end.

When Fletcher gave evasive answers, Grant had the temerity to insist on responsive ones. Even T. Scott Wynn, who'd met with Fletcher the day before the deposition and assured him there would be no trouble, seemed uninterested in derailing Grant from his frontal attack.

In the few other depositions Fletcher had given, the lawyer on his side had defended him with an endless barrage of objections to virtually every question. While Fletcher had never been able to decipher those objections, he noticed that his inquisitors had usually grown tired of the fight and lost their train of thought after a prolonged battle over objections.

Instead of the familiar tactic, Wynn occasionally muttered, "objection form," which did nothing to shake Grant from his line of questioning. When pressed by Fletcher during a break, Wynn explained that the Texas Rules allowed few objections and barred an attorney from making disruptive objections in a deposition. Fletcher found this a thoroughly idiotic rule and made a mental note to refuse further work for attorneys from Texas.

Fletcher was particularly annoyed that he had to endure not only the constant questioning of this lawyer, but the steely glare of Grant's client as well. Haller had not averted his gaze during the deposition, and the unrelenting eye contact from a man with a prosthetic leg who'd recently returned from combat was unnerving. Unfamiliar with the process of a legal deposition, Fletcher was even less accustomed to people being permitted to eyeball him while he was trying to work. Dr. Fletcher's thoughts on this subject were interrupted with the realization that someone was talking to him.

"You keep telling me you were Dr. Perkins' professor in the neurosurgery fellowship here in the eighties," Grant said, "but you haven't told me what that has to do with Dr. Perkins' opinions in this case."

"I explained this before, but you didn't like the answer," Fletcher said with a wave of the hand. "I said Dr. Perkins' results in his last twelve procedures, which I've reviewed, are anomalies and will be demonstrated to be the exception rather than the rule when further cases are undertaken. Dr. Perkins should consider the work we've done here at Bellevue in the last twenty years, including the time he spent here under my tutelage. If he did, I believe he'd conclude that the new laser procedure he's attempting will have no greater success, and no fewer complications, than we've had with our conventional surgery."

"You haven't published any articles criticizing Dr. Perkins' work, have you?" Grant asked.

"No, because Dr. Perkins hasn't published his results, as you well know."

"But Dr. Perkins has shared those results with you, both formally and informally, isn't that true?"

"Yes," Fletcher agreed.

"Then why stay silent about your criticisms?"

Fletcher's mouth curled slightly into a subdued smile. "Who says I'm silent? I'm giving this deposition under oath, sharing my thoughts about Dr. Perkins' study with you."

Fletcher saw Grant pause and the smile curled upward a bit more.

"This deposition won't be peer reviewed, though, will it, doctor?" Grant said.

"That's true."

"And if Dr. Perkins has as much success with his next twelve patients as he's had with the last twelve, you can tell everybody he was your prize student, and none of your doctor buddies will know about this deposition unless I give them a copy, will they?"

The smug look on Fletcher's face turned sour. He hated lawyers. "I, ah, I would never do such a thing," he stammered.

"Want to answer the question, doctor?" Grant said.

An icy stare from Fletcher was the only reply.

Grant flashed a wry smile across the table. "Thanks, doc. I love New York."

# CHAPTER 34

While Grant Mercer flew from New York to D/FW, Lewis Cashman wrapped up another typical day at the helm of Castle Guard Insurance Company. A huge score flipping a stock from an Initial Public Offering, the closing of another deal to provide medical coverage to a Fortune 500 company, and it was time to call it a day. Cashman had intended to fit in a workout, but lost interest as the day wore on. He was now on his way to meet Rebecca McDermott for dinner before heading back to the executive suite. He vowed to limit his drinking and perform better when the time came.

Cashman took a taxi to Pastis, the trendy French café in the meat packing district. The area had undergone a stunning renewal in recent years and was now home to some of the hippest clubs and restaurants on the island. Cashman walked past old buildings recently converted to lofts and condos and reminded himself to check into real estate investments in this part of town.

He entered the restaurant about thirty minutes ahead of his scheduled meeting time with Rebecca, which meant he'd be there nearly an hour before she arrived. Cashman often wondered why she needed to be tardy at all times. Was it extensive preparation time or just a need to have others wait on her? Cashman had a short fuse for such things with most people, but had surprising patience with

Rebecca. With her body and the things she did with it, he figured, she's entitled to be as late as she wants to be.

He sat at the bar and ordered a Ketel One martini. Along with the smooth Dutch vodka, he enjoyed the scenery in the café. The sheer volume of young and beautiful women in Manhattan never ceased to amaze Cashman, and it had become something of a sport for him to take account of the best of the crowd in a particular establishment. He considered all of these women prospects, and had converted the vast majority of his opportunities.

At first, Cashman was surprised at the ease with which he was able to bed women fifteen or twenty years younger than himself. He assumed they'd be more interested in men closer to their own age, particularly those looking for something more casual. He learned, however, that the combination of prestige and wealth in a man his age could be deadly. He suspected the story might be different if he was a mid-level manager at Castle Guard instead of its CEO, but he was sure Henry Kissinger was right. Power is indeed the most reliable aphrodisiac.

After his second martini, which he assured himself would be his last, Cashman realized Rebecca was now fifteen minutes late. With fifteen minutes until she was likely to arrive, he paid a quick visit to the men's room. He stepped to the toilet, annoyed that the rest room lacked a urinal, and unzipped. As he finished his business, he heard the door open and turned to see another patron enter the restroom, close the lock latch on the door, and proceed to the washbasin, whistling a random tune.

The other customer wore a full beard under a Yankees cap and a pair of aviator shades. Cashman thought it odd to see the oversized black pea coat, considering the unseasonably warm weather. With only one sink, Cashman had nowhere else to go and considered for a moment simply walking to the table. He had a cleanliness habit bordering on obsessive-compulsive disorder, though, and simply had to wash his hands before dinner.

After another thirty seconds, however, his patience had worn thin. "You mind, pal?" Cashman asked. "You got somebody waiting."

"Sorry," said the other hand washer, stepping back and gesturing Cashman to the wash basin.

"Thanks," said Cashman. "I'll let you back in when I'm done."

As Cashman ran his hands under the water and pumped the soap into his palm, he heard, "No hurry, Mr. Cashman."

Surprised that the stranger had used his name, Cashman looked up to see the reflection of a hand rising above his head. The momentary uncertainty cost Cashman, who never saw the knife and was unable to move as the five-inch blade sank deep into the soft space at the top of his flabby neck, just under the base of the skull. Cashman died instantly, his spinal cord severed and his brain stem sliced in half by the thrust of the blade. His attacker pinned his body against the counter so he wouldn't immediately slump to the floor.

The killer grabbed a handful of Cashman's thin, graying hair, the tonic leaving a greasy sheen on the vinyl glove, and retracted the knife blade, wiping it on the insurance executive's Armani suit jacket. Lewis Cashman, CEO of Castle Guard Insurance Company, was then allowed to fall unceremoniously to the hard tile floor in front of the washbasin, blood still spilling through the grotesque gash in the back of his neck and arms lying askew at his sides.

Cashman's assailant stepped back and snapped the knife shut, inadvertently slicing through the vinyl glove and opening a small wound in the index finger of the hand holding the knife. Instinctively, the killer brought the hand up, removed the glove, and tried to stanch the bleeding by biting softly on the injured digit.

As the fingers and hand brushed against the false whiskers of the beard, a few hairs pulled free of the adhesive holding them together and fell to the floor. Most dropped into the growing circle of crimson on the checkered floor, but one came to rest straddling the grout seam of the black and white tiles, just outside the sanguine pond surrounding Lewis Cashman's lifeless body.

When the murder weapon was slipped into a jacket pocket a moment later, two drops of blood fell from the incised finger, landing on the tile within inches of the baseboard. Given the blood now spreading into a widening pool around Cashman's head, the two drops were barely noticeable.

With the water still running, the killer clicked open the small lock with an ungloved hand, pulled the door ajar, and walked out into the restaurant past the hostess station. Rebecca McDermott sat in the entry scanning the bar for Lewis Cashman. McDermott is truly exceptional, the killer thought. She certainly won't have any trouble finding another boyfriend.

# CHAPTER 35

Melissa Nance and her two subordinates from the NYPD crime lab arrived thirty minutes after Cashman's final rest room visit. Patrolmen had already closed off the men's room with yellow crime scene tape and had ordered customers to leave the restaurant as soon as possible. With a dead body in the men's room, none had needed encouragement.

The CSI team interviewed the dead man's girlfriend, who unfortunately arrived just in time to find out there would be no romantic dinner on this particular evening. She was initially hysterical, but calmed down enough to say she hadn't seen Cashman since the previous evening and had no information to offer that might help them solve the crime.

Nance questioned Nigel Flatley, a busboy who'd seen a bearded man in a Yankees cap and sunglasses exit the men's room. Even in an eclectic crowd, this particular person seemed out of place to Flatley.

"So you didn't recognize this guy as a regular customer?" asked Nance.

"Like I told those other cops," said a thoroughly disinterested Flatley, "I never saw the guy before. I told my manager what he looked like, and he don't know him, either."

Nance turned to the manager, Sid Jensen. "Anything unusual when you got into the rest room?"

THE PRICE OF LIFE

"Nothing but the stiff," said Jensen. "Now is there anything else? I have to go tell the owner of this place how I let a customer get killed in the john, and did it early enough to lose a whole night's sales. I'll probably be flipping burgers at Mickie D's by tomorrow afternoon."

"Thanks, Mr. Jensen. Just be sure to leave your cell number with the officer." Nance also suspected Jensen would be employed elsewhere in the near future.

With the interviews of potential witnesses out of the way, the crime lab techs went to work in the bathroom. Nance watched carefully as they dusted the porcelain wash basin and brass handles of the faucets for fingerprints. The surfaces were wet, making it impossible to lift a usable print. Next, they searched the basin, the countertop, and the floor in the area of the sink for hair, fibers, or any other physical evidence that might present itself. Unlike their counterparts on television, they didn't douse all lights and use tiny penlights to perform this task.

Nance trained her own flashlight down the wall to the floor, resting the beam on several droplets of blood between the wall and the body. Her training told her the victim's blood had sprayed in that direction when the murder took place, and she expected to see blood spatter. For that reason, she didn't differentiate between the blood drops running from the puddle to the wall and a couple of slightly larger drops just outside the area of the others. Nance ordered a tech to collect a sample from the large blood pool, and authorized cleanup after the sample was collected.

Instead of the blood droplets, Nance focused on two short strands of hair resting in the pool of drying blood. Nance dropped to her knees on the hard tile, holding a magnifier and flashlight. She used a small pair of forceps to collect the hairs and place them into

161

evidence envelopes, taking care to allow her partner to photograph the hairs first, including a couple of shots of her extraction in progress.

As she finished bagging the hairs and marking the envelope, Nance started the process of preparing the body for transport to the morgue. A technician from the coroner's office took an hour to examine the body where it lay, and another twenty to take a couple dozen photographs. The victim's hands were bagged, and plastic wrapped his head to the level of his shirt collar. Finally, the body was placed into a heavy black plastic bag, which in turn was zipped shut before being loaded onto a gurney and wheeled outside to a waiting hearse. Lewis Cashman was dead, but he would talk to the police and to the medical examiner, thanks to the evidence left behind by his killer.

# CHAPTER 36

Sheriff Barlow and Special Agent Thompson spent two days in Austin reviewing evidence from the Sellett murder. They walked the crime scene again and found nothing unexpected. They interviewed Sellett's girlfriend and the couple who had dinner with them on the night of the murder. They viewed Sellett's body with the coroner and reviewed the report from the detective who dusted the scene for fingerprints. No new leads were developed from any of it.

On the way back from lunch, Barlow brought up the report on fibers collected at the scene. "You remember the report said they found human hair at the scene that didn't match the victim?"

"Yeah," Thompson said, "Could have come from anybody, anytime."

"True, but isn't it strange that the hair came from two sources, both female?" asked Barlow. "The report also said that one hair sample was from the victim's jacket, and the other from his hand. The end of the hairs they found in his hand had adhesive on them."

"So our perp wore a fake beard. Most wigs and hairpieces, including fake beards, are made from women's hair."

"But why the two donors?"

"Who knows?" Thompson said. "Word has it Sellett was a player. We're probably lucky there's not hair from three or four women."

"The girlfriend says it was exclusive."

"Don't they all?"

Barlow stifled a laugh. "Maybe the DNA geeks can help us with all that. What do you say we go to the lab and take one more look at Sellett's personal effects before we head back to Fort Worth?"

"Fine." Thompson grunted. "But if we don't find anything, we head out of town before three. Traffic is a bitch in this place late in the afternoon."

Back at the Austin Police Department's crime lab, the two men retrieved two boxes holding Bill Sellett's personal effects from the evidence storage locker. Thompson signed for the boxes and retreated to an examination room, spreading the contents out on the large table.

There was a two-piece Hickey Freeman suit, in a cloth of midnight blue gabardine wool with a faint pinstripe, accompanied by a cotton dress shirt from Joseph Abboud, white background with thin alternating stripes of black and blue. A patterned gold and blue tie, cuff links of solid silver, a black belt with silver buckle, and black square-toed lace-up shoes completed the clothing.

No bracelet or necklace could be found. According to Sellett's girlfriend, he wasn't in the habit of wearing jewelry. The only exceptions were a watch, always expensive, she said, and a class ring. Barlow and Thompson double checked the inventory and the boxes and found no watch, expensive or otherwise. In an envelope extracted from the second box they found a wallet made of coffee-colored alligator skin containing a driver's license and a few membership cards, but no cash or credit cards.

The last item in the box was Sellett's class ring, which declared him to be a graduate of Michigan State University, class of 1981. On the side of the ring, a football player delivered a ferocious stiff arm to an imaginary tackler, the word "CAPTAIN" inscribed on a banner above his head.

"Anybody check these for trace?" Barlow asked.

"Nope," replied Thompson. "They looked at the wallet for prints, but the ring is too small and too rough on the outside to catch any. Inside is clean as a whistle, according to the report."

Barlow grabbed a lighted magnifying glass attached to a gooseneck stand and swung it toward him while flipping the switch. After a moment, he turned to Thompson.

"Maybe we should get a better look at this," he said.

Thompson changed places with the sheriff and peered at the ring with the help of the magnifier. When he turned it to examine the top of the ring bearing the Michigan State crest, he saw what Barlow had discovered. Inside the oval encircling the crest was a speck of what at first glance appeared to be lint. Both men thought it might be skin, silently nodding their agreement. It was barely discernible, even with the aid of the magnifier, but Thompson had seen cases broken open on less.

"Good catch, sheriff," Thompson said. "Let's get this to DNA and see what they come up with."

"How could they miss that?" asked Barlow. "I know we don't have a crime lab and DNA machines in Palo Pinto, but I saw that one."

"Happens more than you'd think," Thompson said. Usually, they check for skin in the ring of a suspect, so they can link him to the victim. They check the victim's nails for skin from an attacker. I guess nobody thought this guy threw any punches. Anyway, this might be a break for the good guys."

"Let's hope so," agreed Barlow, heading out the door to find the nearest DNA specialist.

An hour later, a lab tech in a white coat stuck his head in the room.

"We got the results from the sample off the ring," he said.

"And?" Barlow and Thompson asked in chorus.

"Congratulations, gentlemen," the tech announced. "You just connected Mr. Sellett's death to a barbecue stand."

Thompson and Barlow stared at one another for a moment before Thompson shook his head and asked, "What are you talking about?"

"The guy had pork in his ring. Just a little sauce, too. He should've cleaned it more often, but there's nothing there to help us. Sorry."

"That's okay." Thompson shrugged at the tech. "Let's get the DNA results from the hair samples and the girlfriend into the bureau's computers."

"You got it."

Thompson shook his head. "Let's go, sheriff."

Barlow and Thompson climbed into the agent's Dodge, and were soon on the highway headed north toward Fort Worth. Within fifteen minutes, the skyline of Austin grew smaller in the rearview mirror. The pair sat in silence for a bit, each mulling over the evidence they now had regarding the death of William Sellett. Barlow broke the silence.

"Why did you want to be a cop in the first place?" Barlow asked.

"My dad was a cop," Thompson said. First as a deputy sheriff in Durango, where I was born, then in Denver as a patrolman. He moved to the detective division while I was in high school."

"Is he still there?"

"He and Mom still live in Denver, but he's not on the force anymore," Thompson replied, staring out the windshield through a pair of black Ray-Bans. "One night, while I was playing a high school baseball game, my dad was working undercover to infiltrate a local drug ring. DPD thought they were close to getting him into the circle, and the talk was that they'd get a bunch of convictions thanks to my dad's work."

Thompson heaved a deep sigh. "Instead, the dealers discovered his identity a few days before the meeting and decided to make an example of him. He took five shots in all. The bullet wounds to his chest and shoulder nearly killed him. There was a thirty-minute standoff between the police and the drug dealers. By the time he got to the emergency room, he was unconscious, and he coded three times while they worked on him. Lack of oxygen left his brain impaired, and his motor skills have never been the same. Still sharp as a tack, thank God, and doing better lately. He's on permanent disability leave from the department." Thompson paused. "He's my hero."

Barlow nodded. "I'll bet he is."

The agent drew another breath and started to speak, but was interrupted by his cell phone. "Thompson," he barked.

"It's Carter," said his boss, Special Agent Fred Carter, head of the Fort Worth field office. "Are you still in Austin?"

"No, sir. We're almost to Waco."

"Plans have changed, Thompson," said the boss. "Get yourself on the next flight to New York. And take the sheriff with you."

"What's going on, sir?"

"You know those hair samples from your crime scene in Austin?" asked Carter.

"Yes, sir."

"No ID yet, but we got a perfect match on one of them to DNA recovered from a murder in New York two days ago. The match is from the Austin hairs with the adhesive. Looks like the same guy's doing business in New York. Go to the Manhattan field office and check in with Special Agent Delgado. He'll have everything you need."

"On our way now, sir," said Thompson before disconnecting the call.

"On our way where, Tonto?" asked Barlow.

"New York," Thompson replied as he accelerated. "And I'm Kimo Sabe. You're Tonto."

# CHAPTER 37

Tonto and Kimo Sabe arrived at the New York field office early the next morning, as instructed. They were met by Special Agent Oscar Delgado, who took them immediately to a lab lined with large flat-screen computer monitors. To Barlow, it looked like mission control at NASA. Introductions were made all around.

"Here you go, boys," said Delgado. "This DNA from the hair sample recovered from our crime scene at the restaurant is a match to the DNA from your murder in Austin. Who does it belong to?"

"Don't know yet," said Thompson. "But Sheriff Barlow here thinks we may have a third murder by the same guy."

"Is that right?" asked Delgado, glaring at Barlow. He obviously didn't share Thompson's esteem for local law enforcement.

"Well, that's my theory," Barlow said weakly.

"Come on, Tonto," Thompson urged. "Delgado here isn't as big a prick as you think. Give him a chance to show you that a Yankee can actually listen instead of just talking all the time."

Delgado silently turned his glare toward Thompson, looking like he wanted to give him a straight right hand to the head.

Barlow arched an eyebrow toward Delgado. "You two friends?"

"I wouldn't say that," Delgado said. "When your boy Will graduated from the Academy, they sent him to me in Miami. I guess you could say I showed him the ropes."

"More like I saved your ass," Thompson said.

Delgado threw his head back and let out a hearty laugh. "You're killing me, Thompson. Why don't you start your story, sheriff, before the lies get out of hand."

Barlow hitched up his jeans. "Here goes. First victim was mine, Senator Ken Dunbar, outside my hometown near Possum Kingdom Lake."

Delgado snickered at the name. Thompson shot him a look of his own and told Barlow to go ahead.

"Anyway, we looked at that one with the assistance of the Bureau in Fort Worth, which is where I met Special Agent Thompson. We had no evidence to work with, but a few days later I read in the paper about a lawyer getting killed down in Austin."

"Mr. Sellett, who apparently liked pork ribs," said Delgado.

"Exactly." Barlow nodded. "There was no apparent connection from the evidence, but Dunbar worked on a pretty controversial piece of medical malpractice legislation a few years ago. The article in the paper mentioned that Sellett was involved in the same legislation. So I asked a few of the regulars at the lake, and it turns out Sellett and Dunbar were pretty tight, spent weekends on the lake together and all. And I thought, that's funny, a couple of friends murdered within a couple of weeks of each other, so I went to see my good friend Special Agent Thompson."

"Kimo Sabe to you," said Thompson.

"To Kimo Sabe," Barlow said with a grin. "We went to Austin, where they have hair samples from the crime scene. We discovered that the same hair was recovered from the scene of a murder in New

THE PRICE OF LIFE

York City, and it seems pretty clear that the New York murder is connected to the Austin murder, which I think is connected to the Possum Kingdom murder."

"Well, Tonto," said Delgado, shooting his own look at Thompson, "it turns out you may be onto something. Our victim here is Lewis Cashman, the CEO of Castle Guard Insurance Company. Know anything about them?"

"No," said Barlow, seeing that Thompson was also shaking his head, "Should we?"

"Castle Guard is a pretty big player in the medical insurance market," said Delgado. "Cashman took over almost two years ago. Everyone there loves him. Profits are way up, claims payments are way down, and they have a ten-year deal with the Defense Department to provide insurance benefits to active duty soldiers and their families. Life is good."

"Is there a connection or not?" Barlow was growing impatient.

"Sure looks that way, sheriff," said Delgado. "Your victim, Mr. Sellett, was Castle Guard's lawyer. Did their lobbying in Austin, and in Congress, too. He was a heavy hitter."

Barlow and Thompson cast curious glances at one another. They now had Sellett connected with both of the other victims. Barlow let out a low whistle between his teeth.

"You said it," said Delgado. "The boss wants you to go through the evidence on the Cashman murder, see if there's anything else that sticks out. Then, you two boys can head back to Texas."

"Show us where to look," said Thompson.

Delgado stuck out his hand toward Barlow. "Nice work, sheriff," he said. "Glad you saw that story and decided to bother my friend here."

"Yeah," replied Barlow. "He's usually right, especially in this case."

"Oh yeah?" Delgado asked. "What did he get right here?"

"You're really not as big a prick as I thought you were."

Delgado tightened his grip and pulled Barlow close, a fearsome scowl crossing his face. Suddenly, he broke out into a raucous laugh and slapped Barlow on the shoulder.

"Come on, boys," he said. "Let's try to put all this together."

THE PRICE OF LIFE

# CHAPTER 38

After reviewing the case book for the rest of the morning, the two FBI agents and the Texas sheriff took a walk across Lower Manhattan to visit the restaurant crime scene. Thanksgiving decorations adorned light posts and storefronts. Sunshine glistened from every building while a slight chill announced the impending arrival of winter weather.

A couple of blocks from the café, Delgado treated to lunch from a street vendor. The idea of eating a meal prepared on a metal cart was totally foreign to Ronnie Clyde Barlow, and he recoiled at Delgado's suggestion.

"You're kidding, right?" Barlow asked as they walked up to the vendor. "You really expect me to eat something whipped up in the middle of a sidewalk in New York City?"

"Just leave the ordering to me," Delgado said. "I promise it'll be at least as good as pickled pig's feet, or whatever you country boys eat."

Thompson shrugged at Barlow, who reluctantly nodded in Delgado's direction. Moments later, Delgado ordered gyros, with tomatoes and onions and extra tzadziki. Other than the vegetables, Barlow had no idea what he was about to eat. Fortunately, it didn't matter that he couldn't pronounce it. The rotisserie beef and lamb, sliced from a cone-shaped hunk of meat spinning slowly on a turntable next to a heating element, was served in warm pita bread with the onions and tomatoes. The topping of tzadziki was a sauce of yogurt and cucumbers, mixed with a bit of garlic and a splash of olive oil. The result was unlike anything Barlow had ever eaten, and just melted in his mouth.

Delgado and Thompson watched with glee as Barlow's expression turned from fear to curiosity to amazement with each bite. The best moment came when a thick glob of tzadziki spilled over the edge of the pita and landed, unbeknownst to the sheriff, on the only clean shirt Barlow had with him. Delgado would have laughed all afternoon, but Thompson took pity on the sheriff and spoiled the fun after a minute or so by pointing out the mishap to Barlow and handing him a napkin.

Once at the restaurant, the men took a half hour or so to get a thorough look at the dining area, the bar, and the rest rooms. The scene had been completely scoured within a few hours after being released by the NYPD, and there was virtually no hope that any evidence had survived. Barlow and the two FBI men stood in the cramped space near the washbasin, all three uncomfortable with the lack of room to maneuver. Barlow stood nearest to the door, slowly scanning the walls and floor for anything of value to the investigation. As he faced the inside of the door, his eyes came to rest on the metal locking mechanism attached to the door itself, with the receptacle for the latch screwed into the wood door frame.

"Anybody dust this for prints?" he asked.

"Yeah," Delgado replied without turning around. "They got the doorknob and the door. Just a couple of smudges. Nothing we could use."

"Not the knob," Barlow protested. "I'm talking about this latch."

Delgado and Thompson both turned, and Delgado flipped open his case file to the report regarding fingerprint gathering and analysis. He scanned the page quickly.

"Nope," he said, reading through the report a second time. "No prints from the latch. It wasn't even dusted."

"Got a flashlight?" asked Barlow. The FBI agent quickly produced a small light from his jacket pocket.

Barlow shone the beam of the instrument directly on the latch. He silently cursed as he strained his eyes to look for evidence of a fingerprint and swore he'd get some reading glasses as soon as he got back home. With help from the light and a moment for his eyes to adjust, he saw the telltale swirl of a fingerprint.

"Hello," he said softly. "Boys, look what I found."

Both agents leaned closer, and each saw the print as clearly as Barlow had. Delgado had his phone out within seconds and dialed the field office to request a crime lab tech. Within thirty minutes, the tech had lifted the print and was headed back to the field office with what they hoped was a piece of evidence that would break open the case.

"Nice catch, Sheriff," said Delgado as they walked out of the restaurant and toward his government-issued Ford. "I can't believe the NYPD guys missed it."

"In their defense, Agent Delgado, it wasn't locked when they examined the crime scene, and I doubt whether anybody would have thought about it," Barlow said. "I wouldn't have figured the door would have a lock until I noticed that the bathroom is a one-holer."

Delgado cocked his head to one side. "What are you talking about?"

"Sheriff Barlow here thought the management might want to give somebody a way to use the head without having somebody else walk in on them," Thompson said. "I didn't notice that, either, but then I didn't go in there to pee."

"We'll run that print through IAFIS, and I'll let you know what I find," said Delgado. "Meantime, you boys want a ride to the airport?"

"Sure thing," said Thompson as they crossed the sidewalk. "See there, Sheriff? I told you Delgado's not such a prick."

Delgado shot Thompson a smile, and the finger, as he slid behind the wheel and fired up the Ford.

Thompson chuckled. "Maybe I'm wrong."

# CHAPTER 39

As Barlow and Thompson waited in the terminal at Newark airport, Delgado called to share the results of the fingerprint analysis from IAFIS. Created in 1999, the Integrated Automated Fingerprint Identification System is the national fingerprint history system maintained by the FBI. Prior to the introduction of IAFIS, fingerprint checks could take up to three months. IAFIS provides automated fingerprint search capabilities, latent search capability, electronic image storage, and electronic exchange of fingerprints and responses. When state and local law enforcement agencies submit fingerprints electronically through IAFIS, they receive electronic responses within two hours.

The fingerprints in IAFIS are gathered by local law enforcement when criminal suspects are arrested and booked. Prints from all ten fingers, known as the ten-print, are collected by the local police and forwarded to the appropriate state-wide agency, which in turn forwards the electronic files to IAFIS. Some federal jobs and civilian positions require fingerprints as part of the application process, but for the most part IAFIS is populated with the fingerprints of criminals.

"We got a good print," Delgado reported. "But we didn't find a match in IAFIS, and it didn't come from the victim. Maybe it'll come in handy when we collar a suspect. Anyway, you guys have a safe trip back to the Wild, Wild West."

"Thanks," Thompson said. "And Sheriff Barlow says thanks again for lunch."

"Bad news?" Barlow asked.

"Bottom line is whoever left the print on that latch had never had fingerprints submitted to IAFIS," Thompson replied with a shrug. "We have a print, but without a match it won't lead us to the killer."

Having been through the evidence in New York without cracking the case, the Lone Ranger and his trusty sidekick were back on a plane bound for Texas by six. As they sat, Barlow ran through his theory with Thompson.

"Dunbar is connected to Sellett by the tort reform bill they passed. And Cashman is connected to Sellett by Castle Guard. I can't figure out a direct link between Cashman and Dunbar, and I can't fill in the blank on who connects them all. But doesn't it seem to you that all three have somebody or something in common?"

"Sure does," Thompson agreed. "The DNA will do that. It would be too coincidental to have the same DNA at two crime scenes so far apart. But we're missing the who, and without someone to compare the DNA samples to, we'll have to find him some other way."

"Let's see if there's someone else out there who can help us,"

"What do you mean?"

"We need to get something in the press talking about a connection between the murders," said Barlow. "Give the public some information, and maybe somebody will have something else that will put us over the top. Hell, it worked once, why not again?"

After landing, the men went straight to the Fort Worth field office. Together, they wrote a story for release in the Sunday editions of *The Fort Worth Star Telegram* and *The Dallas Morning News*:

*Violent crime is uncommon in Palo Pinto County. The murder of State Senator Ken Dunbar was the first homicide investigation for Sheriff Ronnie Clyde Barlow in more than four years. Now, the sheriff is involved in the investigation of the killing of a lawyer in Austin, and may soon be involved in another murder investigation outside the state.*

*Austin police sources confirm that Barlow has worked with them and with other law enforcement agencies on a possible connection between the murder of Dunbar, a Republican from Temple, and William Sellett, a lawyer and lobbyist from Austin with political ties to Dunbar. Sellett was killed last weekend at his home in the fashionable Westlake Hills section of Austin.*

*A seemingly unrelated homicide in New York City has become a part of the investigation. Lewis Cashman was killed in the men's room of a Manhattan restaurant on the evening of November 18th, only a few days after the Sellett murder.*

*A spokesman for the FBI confirmed that the agency has offered its assistance in the investigations, and that there is evidence linking the murder of Cashman, CEO of Castle Guard Insurance Company, to those of the victims in Texas. The spokesman declined to elaborate on exactly what evidence links the crimes. He said the Bureau is asking for the public to contact*

> them with any helpful information. The FBI can be contacted at local field offices, which can be found on the FBI website at www.fbi.gov.

"Not bad," Barlow said as he proofed the article. "You like to fish?"

"Nope," said Thompson. "I like to catch fish."

# CHAPTER 40

On the Tuesday after Thanksgiving, Ed Haller found himself in his lawyer's office with Julie. Grant had called and asked them to come in to discuss something of the highest importance, and said it must be covered in person and not on the phone. Julie had quizzed Ed extensively on the drive into Fort Worth, but her husband swore he had no idea what could be going on.

"Thanks for coming in," said Grant as he walked into the conference room, a folder tucked under one arm. "How about something to drink?"

"We're fine," Haller said. "What's all this about, Mr. Mercer?"

"You know we're set for trial right after the first of the year," Grant said.

"What now?" Haller asked. "Are they trying to push back the trial?"

"No, Ed. They don't want a trial. They've agreed to settle the case."

Grant's words hung in the air as he looked back and forth at his clients. Only the sound of the building's heating system disturbed the sudden silence.

"But, Grant, we haven't even made a demand." This time, it was Julie Haller's turn. "I don't get it."

Grant reached into the folder and pulled out a sheaf of papers and an envelope. He put the papers on the table, then opened the envelope flap and withdrew a check. "They sent this check for $250,000, the most we could ever get from them, along with these settlement papers."

Julie looked up through the tears welling in her eyes. "That's it?" she asked. "It's over?"

"We have to sign these papers. Basically, they say we're releasing Dr. Purser and his group from all liability. They admit no negligence, and we agree to dismiss the lawsuit and never bring it up again. We'll deposit this check, and about a week later I'll have a check for you after deducting our fees and expenses. Once that's done, yes ma'am, it'll be over."

"What do you mean, they admit no negligence?" Haller growled. "Why else would they agree to pay without a trial?"

Grant turned slowly to look at his client. "It's simple, Ed. Even if we won at a trial, they wouldn't admit negligence. They'd just say the jury didn't understand the issues and decided the case against the evidence. With this agreement, we don't say he wasn't negligent. In fact, we have experts who say he was. It's just that his group and his insurance company want to be able to say they settled the case as a business decision instead of admitting that Purser did anything wrong. This is what happens in all these cases. It's a compromise."

Another long silence ensued as Haller and Julie looked at each other, then at Grant, and at each other again. Julie turned toward Grant, but Haller stood and walked away from the table, looking through the window toward the horizon.

"Congratulations, Mr. Mercer," Haller said through clenched teeth.

"I usually congratulate my clients when we settle a case," said Grant. "But it doesn't feel right to use that word here. Instead, let me say this. I think you did the right thing by your daughter. She couldn't speak for herself, so you spoke for her. We did as well as we could with this case. I realize it's not the same as winning, but I hope you and your family can complete your grieving and live your life with the memory of Jennifer as she was before she got sick. I hope this can be the end of a painful part of your life."

As he finished speaking, Grant reached into his pocket and handed Julie his handkerchief to wipe away the tears now streaming down her face. She put her arms around Grant's neck, hugging him tightly.

"Thank you so much," she whispered in his ear. "I don't think I could have handled a trial. I just wanted this to be over. I never expected them to do this."

Grant looked over her shoulder to her husband, who stood and waited for his wife to release her embrace of their attorney. For all the emotion flowing from Julie, her husband revealed no sadness, no relief, no outward sign that he was satisfied with the settlement. To the contrary, what Grant saw was the anger and frustration of a man who obviously didn't believe that justice had been served. Haller shook his head and slowly turned back toward them.

Grant stepped forward and shook Haller's hand, thankful when Haller stopped just short of snapping bones. Haller said nothing, barely nodding at Grant during the handshake before disengaging to take his wife in his arms. Grant gave them a moment, then led them through the signatures of the releases and the back side of the check before walking them to the elevator lobby.

After bidding farewell to his clients, Grant walked down the hall and broke the news to his partner, thinking Charlie Montgomery would be elated to get a maximum recovery without the trouble and expense of a trial. The reaction was quite different.

"Great." Montgomery snorted sarcastically. "Last I saw you had more than 300 hours on the case. That's about six weeks of steady billing for me. And what's the referral fee? A quarter of it? I'm not crazy about $250 an hour when we had no guarantee of being paid. Hell, the best news is that it's over."

"Want to know how the clients feel about it?" asked Grant without enthusiasm.

"Not particularly," said Montgomery, picking up the phone to signal the end of the conversation.

Grant knew he should have expected Montgomery's reaction, but it still stung. For all his positive traits, Grant's partner had long forgotten that fees, rates, and billable hours were factors when considering the success of a case, but weren't the only factors.

Grant wondered whether Montgomery would feel differently if he knew the sacrifices made by Ed Haller, if he'd seen the look on Julie's face, if he'd heard the relief in her voice as she thanked him for his work and for sparing her family the angst of a prolonged trial about the death of her daughter. Probably not, Grant thought. He decided it didn't matter whether his partner appreciated those things. Grant did.

As he walked back to his office with $250,000 in his hand, Grant thought of Ed Haller and his reaction to the news of the settlement. He'd seen stoic men before, men who refused to allow emotion to come to the surface in the face of tragedy. Eventually, they'd all shown cracks, some more than others. None in his experience had kept it smothered like Haller, which disturbed Grant.

Haller was a Marine. He'd seen and done things that would harden the softest heart. But he'd lost his daughter, whom he clearly loved more than life itself. Grant had been prepared to offer condolences to Haller, as ludicrous as that thought sounded.

Over the years, Grant had improved at comforting his clients, thanks to parenthood and the familiarity with the feeling of loving someone else so deeply that the thought of life without that person was unbearable. He'd tried to use that feeling to let his clients know he understood what they were going through, even if he hadn't been in the same position himself.

With Haller, Grant knew there was no way he could effectively convey his sympathy without sounding shallow and trite. When the moment came, Haller simply hadn't needed any sympathy, and Grant had been spared the embarrassment of trying. He should have been happy that the case was finished, but a nagging sense of apprehension wouldn't let go.

# CHAPTER 41

Within a few days, the check cleared the bank. Grant distributed the money to his law firm for fees and expenses, to Chris Turner for referral fees, and to his clients for the remainder of the settlement funds. He was back in his office, taking a few minutes toward the end of the afternoon to figure out which cases he would work on next, when he heard a tap on his door.

"Got a minute?" Leslie asked.

"Come on in."

Leslie sat in a side chair, legs crossed. "I'm sorry I missed all the excitement with the Haller case."

"Don't sweat it," Grant said. "You needed the vacation. We didn't expect it to happen so fast."

"How are Ed and Julie?" she asked.

"Just like you think they'd be. Relieved it's over, I guess, but they still don't understand how that can be all we get, especially Ed."

"I gather Mr. Montgomery's about as keen on the settlement as Ed?"

"You could say that, but for different reasons." Grant was eager to change the subject. "What's up with you?"

Leslie's brow furrowed. "Did you read the Sunday paper? The Sunday before Thanksgiving, I mean."

"I don't know. Why?"

"Some guy in New York, name of Cashman, was murdered a couple of weeks ago," Leslie said. Somebody stabbed him in a restaurant in Manhattan. An article in the *Star Telegram* says he was the CEO of Castle Guard. You remember them?"

Grant bristled. "They're the pricks who wouldn't pay for Jennifer Haller's surgery."

Leslie nodded slowly as the silence persisted. "Apparently, the cops think there's a connection between that case and the murders of Ken Dunbar and Bill Sellett. He was the lobbyist from Austin."

"I know who he was," Grant said. "I spilled a drink on his tuxedo at the Cattle Baron's ball. Why do they think Cashman is connected to the two cases down here?"

"The article didn't say that, but it did quote your buddy Ronnie Clyde Barlow. He says they're working with the FBI, and they want help from the public."

"Do you have that article?" Grant asked.

"You can pull it up on the Internet."

Grant turned to his computer and went to the newspaper's website, where he quickly found the story about the possibility of a connection between the murders of Ken Dunbar, Bill Sellett, and Lewis Cashman.

The article gave the date of the Cashman murder as November 18. Grant moved the article to the bottom of the screen and clicked an icon for his calendar, checking his activities for the previous month. Sure enough, the 18th was the date of the deposition of Dr. Fletcher at Bellevue Hospital in Manhattan. Grant read the article twice, each time hoping his eyes were deceiving him and the date would somehow appear differently on the next read. It didn't.

"Didn't you know Sellett before the Cattle Baron's ball?" Leslie asked.

"No," said Grant, "but I knew of him. His name was all over tort reform for years."

"Senator Dunbar was a tort reformer, too," said Leslie.

Grant's stomach pulled into a tight, painful knot. "Are you thinking what I'm thinking?"

"Ed researched all these guys, right?"

"Actually, it was Julie who did the research, but she shared it with Ed."

Leslie frowned. "He knew about Sellett and Dunbar. Getting to them would be easy. He didn't like how Castle Guard treated his family."

"He was in New York with me on the date of Cashman's murder."

Leslie nodded. "Sheriff Barlow's a friend of yours, isn't he?"

"I don't know that I'd say we're friends, but I've known him fifteen years."

"You should call him," Leslie said.

"Barlow's trying to solve three murders, Leslie." Grant stood and paced. "I can't hand him my client."

"Grant," said Leslie quietly. "There's somebody else."

"Purser." Grant stopped pacing. "What can I tell Barlow that won't point right at Ed Haller?"

"Maybe he can tell you whether we're on the right track. Maybe you won't have to tell him everything, but you can't sit by and do nothing about Purser."

Grant picked up the phone and dialed the number to the Palo Pinto County Sheriff's office.

"Barlow," was the one-word response after three rings.

"Sheriff Barlow, it's Grant Mercer."

"Well, this is a surprise," Barlow said. "What can I do for you today?"

"Let me get right to it. I just read the article in the *Star Telegram*. It says you're investigating Senator Dunbar's death and the possible connections with Bill Sellett and now this other case in New York."

"Why are you calling me?" asked Barlow.

"Maybe I can help you with that," replied Grant, nervously eyeing Leslie. "Can you meet me in Mineral Wells, at the Wagon Wheel, in an hour?"

"Sure, Grant," Barlow said. "You want to tell me what this is about?"

"I'll do that in person." Grant knew better than to expect Barlow to discuss the case in detail on the telephone. "See you at the Wagon Wheel. One hour."

"Anything I can do?" asked Leslie as Grant hung up.

"Go home," he said. "And forget we had this conversation."

# CHAPTER 42

Grant hustled to the Tahoe and was on the freeway in minutes. As he drove, Grant tried to figure out how to get Barlow to tell him about the details of his investigation without having to fully reciprocate. Barlow probably didn't know about the Castle Guard connection to the Haller case, which would be to Grant's advantage.

He walked into the Wagon Wheel and saw Barlow sitting in a brown naugahide booth in the back corner, sipping coffee from a small mug. Neither man made a move to gesture to the other. Grant slid into the booth seat across from the sheriff while ordering black coffee from the waitress, who seemed a bit miffed that neither of her customers expressed interest in eating.

"Howdy," said Grant.

"Did you get me to drive an hour just for a cup of Janice's coffee?" Barlow asked.

"I guess we'll find out, won't we?"

"All right then, counselor," said Barlow, peering curiously at Grant. "Let's find out now."

"The story in the paper says the three murders are being investigated together. I may have something that'll help you, but I need you to fill in the gaps for me about your investigation so I know whether I'm telling you something you need to know."

"Okay, Grant, we'll play it your way for now. I can't say why, but I can tell you that the Cashman and Sellett murders were done by the same killer." Barlow leaned back and took a swallow of the harsh, thick coffee. "I was in New York a few days ago, taking a look at the evidence there. They found some hair at the scene that didn't belong to Cashman. When we compared it to the DNA from hair we recovered from Mr. Sellett down in Austin, it was a dead solid match. No hits in CODIS, though. You know what that is?"

"Sure," said Grant. "I watch CSI. It's the database for DNA."

"Almost," said Barlow. "It's the FBI's index of DNA profiles. It doesn't have names, just DNA data. If we get a hit in CODIS, we have to get a suspect matched by another DNA analysis. But like I said, we know that whoever left the DNA on Cashman is the same person who left it on Sellett.

"Anyway, we don't have any evidence from any of the scenes to link Cashman or Sellett to Ken Dunbar's death, but we know Dunbar and Sellett were friends. They got to know each other while Sellett was pushing tort reform at the legislature."

"Senator Dunbar was the sponsor of the bill," Grant said.

"Right," Barlow said. "So I looked at this, and I saw three things connected, not two. Castle Guard Insurance, the company Cashman worked for, was a client of Sellett's. He and Cashman did some socializing together when Sellett was in New York."

Grant let out a long breath.

"I can't connect Dunbar and Cashman directly," Barlow said, "but Sellett is the common denominator here. I figure there's a reason one guy would want all of these people dead. I just haven't figured it out yet."

Grant felt a cold rivulet of sweat slide from the base of his neck down his spine. He hoped Barlow couldn't tell from his shallow breathing that he was terrified. He had to get the hell out of there, and quickly, but he had to be careful not to alarm the sheriff.

Grant watched Barlow speak, unable to hear the words, for what seemed like an eternity. He felt nauseated and dizzy, and was sure his forehead bore beads of sweat from his hairline to his eyebrows. Suddenly, he heard Barlow say his name.

"What?" Grant fought to control his stampeding heart.

"I asked why you called me about the case."

Grant cleared his throat and hoped his voice wouldn't shake as he spoke. "I handled a case not too long ago involving Castle Guard Insurance. I've never heard of Mr. Cashman, but I figured I might be able to help if I had the whole story. I guess not, now that you've told me about the case."

"That's it?" Barlow asked. "You had to drive out here to tell me you had a case with Castle Guard?"

"That's it," Grant lied. "Sorry I wasted your time."

Barlow shrugged, still trying to read Grant's face. "It was worth a try. I know you'll call me if you figure something out."

Grant watched Barlow studying him over his coffee mug. The sheriff was clearly suspicious, but didn't press.

Grant heard his cell phone ring and hurriedly snapped it open. His wife wanted to know when he'd be home.

"Sorry, Sam," said Grant, relieved for the interruption and the excuse to leave. "I forgot to call earlier. I'm wrapping up a meeting, then I'm on my way."

"Where are you?" Samantha asked.

"Oh, yeah," said Grant. "I forgot about the concert tonight. I should just be able to make it. Okay. Love you, too."

Grant hung up while Samantha kept talking. "I have to go," he said to Barlow. "My daughter has a choir concert tonight. Lucky my wife reminded me. You never want to get in trouble with a fifteen-year-old girl."

"That's good advice," Barlow said, rising and offering his card. "Sorry you had to come all the way out here on a week night, Grant. Here's my card. Home and cell are on the back. If you hear anything you think will help us in the investigation, give me a call."

"Sure thing," said Grant, laying a five dollar bill on the table. "The coffee's on me."

It was all Grant could do to keep from sprinting out the front door. It took equal discipline not to gun the engine and squeal the tires on the way out of the parking lot. Somehow, he kept his speed at the limit of thirty-five through town. Once on the highway, however, he accelerated rapidly and was soon doing eighty.

# CHAPTER 43

Dr. Robert Purser left his clinic in Fort Worth's hospital district after a thoroughly uneventful day. Christmas was approaching, and the air held the brisk, refreshing quality absent at other times of the year.

Purser had planned on a busy Christmas holiday preparing for trial of the Haller case in early January. His attorney had harassed him relentlessly to consent to a settlement from the insurance company, and Purser had ultimately relented. He wasn't pleased with surrendering, but his schedule would be far less stressful without a looming trial. Purser would finish the work week and enjoy three weeks of vacation, including ten days skiing at his condo in Vail.

Thoughts of packed powder and after-ski toddies brought a smile to Purser's face as he accelerated onto the freeway. His expression turned decidedly sour when he noticed the low fuel light on the instrument panel of his new Bentley. Strange, he thought, since he clearly recalled filling the tank on Saturday morning.

Purser swore to himself. "That kid has to stop driving my car." His incorrigible seventeen-year-old son was known to borrow the Bentley without asking.

Purser took the next exit and pulled into a Shell station. He swiped his American Express Platinum card and inserted the nozzle into the receptacle on the left rear fender of the shiny black automobile. As he did, a white cargo van pulled up at same pump on the other side of the fuel island. The driver climbed out, wearing a fatigue jacket of olive drab camouflage and a Dallas Cowboys cap, and reached toward the pump with a credit card. Purser looked up when he heard the other driver curse and heard what sounded like a low string of obscenities.

The van driver then stepped around the pump and walked uncomfortably close to Purser before taking three paper towels from the dispenser attached to the post, mumbling a quick "Sorry."

"Don't worry about it," Purser said.

As the man turned around with the paper towels in one hand, he withdrew a small aerosol dispenser from his jacket pocket and sprayed a fine mist of anesthetic agents into Purser's face. Within a second, the combination of halothane and nitrous oxide took effect, and Purser fell into the stranger's arms. The other driver lunged forward, bracing himself against the driver's door of the Bentley for leverage. He dragged Purser to the side door of the van, which was already open, and laid the doctor inside.

# CHAPTER 44

Purser's Bentley stood at the pump, still receiving fuel. The man quickly stepped to the hose and shut it off, replacing the nozzle in its holster in the front of the pump. Tearing the receipt from the slot in the machine, the stranger slid into the driver's seat and pulled the Bentley out of the gas station and into a parking spot at the Whataburger next door. He then hurried back to the van, climbed in, and drove away from the station. The entire process took less than a minute and was witnessed by absolutely nobody.

From the Shell station, the man drove the van west past the loop and out of Fort Worth. After twenty minutes, he took the first exit at Willow Park and drove south to Mulberry Street, where he turned right. A mile later, he turned into the parking lot of an industrial park, making his way slowly to the space on the end, which had a garage bay as a part of the warehouse. He depressed the button of a remote control to lift the rollup door, then pulled the van into the bay before hitting the remote again and killing the engine. Once the door closed, he retrieved the unconscious doctor from the cargo area of the van and carried him to the corner of the bay, where he efficiently stripped him of his expensive suit and its accessories.

The space had previously been used for high-end truck and van conversions, and suited his needs perfectly. The owner had been completely disinterested in any details, and had accepted cash for three months' rent in advance without the need for a lease. There was a small office and a smaller reception area in the front, which he didn't use. The remainder of the space was just concrete floor and walls.

He'd customized the place with a metal surgical table equipped with leather restraints. The table was also fitted with retractable boards, so that either or both of his subject's arms could be retracted away from his body and held firm for any procedure. The table itself was placed at a forty-five-degree angle to the floor and welded to a set of iron struts cut specifically for his purposes. A wide leather strap provided restraint across the chest of the subject, and an additional, smaller strap would be available for use as a halo if restricting the motion of the head was deemed necessary.

The man placed the naked physician on the table and cinched the chest strap, holding the doctor in place while he applied the leather straps to his ankles, thighs, wrists, and elbows. He checked his watch. The doctor would be awake in another ten minutes on his own, or sooner with counteracting medication to speed the process. He decided he'd be patient, and would use the time to set up his tools.

He began by hooking up the electrical leads emanating from behind the bed, where they attached to an electrical distribution board to control the voltage sent through the wires. Each of the twelve leads snaked up the table, six per side, and was tipped with a small, razor-sharp metallic clip to allow placement virtually anywhere on the body. The control panel sat on a cart at the edge of the bed and contained a set of knobs the man could reach with ease.

He carefully placed each clip in a spot he knew would cause a great deal of pain, but would not itself render Purser unconscious. When the placement of the clips was finished, Purser wore clips in the earlobe, at the base of the skull, under the nipple, in the groin, and in the webbing between Purser's toes.

Next, he took stock of the surgical tools collected over the past few days. A couple of different styles of scalpels and scissors, along with a variety of probes and picks, were arrayed on a tray on the tableside cart near the voltage controls. A few syringes attached to hypodermic needles lay beside the tools, each containing a mixture of drugs designed to induce consciousness or unconsciousness, depending on the need of the moment.

As the doctor slowly came to, the man finished his inventory and drew a deep breath. He was ready.

"Where am I?" asked Purser with a thick tongue.

"Ah, good evening, doctor," said the man. "Feeling a little sluggish, are we?"

Without further comment, he reached to the table and picked up a syringe of Narcan, a powerful stimulant used to counteract the effects of prescription painkillers, and injected its contents into the doctor's shoulder. Within seconds, Purser was completely awake and struggling against the restraints.

"Let me out of here, goddammit," he screamed.

The man lifted a scalpel and held it close to the Purser's eyes. "Calm down, doctor," he said politely.

The sight of the sharpened surgical instrument had the desired effect, and Purser immediately quieted, his eyes widening. The man reached back to the table and turned two knobs to half power. Purser screamed as electricity coursed into the flesh above his neck and under his right nipple. After twenty seconds, Purser's nemesis decided this was enough for the first shock treatment, and returned the knobs to the off position. Purser stopped screaming.

"Hurts, doesn't it?" asked the man, leaning close to Purser's face.

"What the hell is this about?" Purser stammered between labored breaths. "If it's money you want, tell me how much. I'll get it."

Knobs were spun again, this time delivering voltage to Purser's groin and feet. Purser screamed as the agony continued for thirty seconds, at which time the man calmly returned the dials to zero.

Purser's brow beaded with sweat, and his breath came in short, ragged bursts. "Please stop," he cried. "I'll give you whatever you want, I promise."

"There's nothing I want from you," the man replied as he turned the controls for the leads attached to the man's nipples and groin once more. The indicators on the dials spun to eight on their scale of ten.

Purser screamed again. The smell of burning flesh filled the room.

"No more," he pleaded over and over again.

"Maybe this will feel better," said the man as he turned off the current and lifted his scalpel.

He felt scant resistance as the knife entered Purser's skin, circling the clip attached to his nipple and excising the flesh cleanly. He held the chunk of tissue in front of Purser's eyes as it swayed hypnotically back and forth on thin strands of wire. After a momentary pause, pain signals reached Purser's brain and the screaming began for real.

"No?" asked the man, feigning concern. "Sorry about that. I thought you said the electricity hurt."

After a minute or so, Purser's shrieking became less fervent, replaced by labored breathing and gentle sobbing. He tried to talk, but was unable to form words. As soon as Purser started to speak, the

man reached to the side of the doctor's head with the scalpel and removed the upper half of his left earlobe with a single swipe. Again, Purser wailed and strained against the straps. They were tight, and his bucking moved the table only slightly without loosening the restraints.

"What do you want from me?" Purser choked, tears and sweat streaming down his face.

"I want my daughter back," the man said. "But you can't do that, can you, Dr. Purser?"

Purser's head spun to face his captor. "But I don't have your daughter."

"I don't, either, thanks to you."

"I don't know what you're talking about," yelled Purser. "Who's your daughter?"

"My daughter was Jennifer Haller," he said, removing his ballcap. "You killed her because you wouldn't pay enough attention to order a simple test."

"You're Jennifer's father?" Purser gasped.

Haller nodded silently.

"Please, Mr. Haller," Purser begged. "I'm sorry for the loss of your daughter. I'd give anything if I could go back and order the CT scan."

"It's too late for that, isn't it, doctor?" Haller's face was inches from Purser's, his breath hot on the doctor's sweaty, pale skin.

"I know," Purser said. "Believe me, I know. Since I learned of your daughter's death, I've retraced my steps in her case hundreds of times. I don't know why I didn't order the test. I just didn't think it was that serious."

"Bullshit," Haller roared. "You screwed the pooch, and my daughter paid with her life."

"I'm so sorry." Purser sobbed. "Really I am. But killing me won't do any good. It won't bring your daughter back to life. It'll just make things harder for you."

"You're right," Haller muttered. "But my life is over anyway. I died when Jennifer died. I'm her father, and I was supposed to protect her. Instead, I was on the other side of the planet, killing people I don't know and who never did anything to me so contractors can build roads and buildings in the Middle East, and we can buy cheap gasoline for our SUV's. I watched men in my command get shot and blown up, and had my own leg blown off. Now I'll be discharged from the Corps, and the government will tell me *sayonara*, lots of luck, and expect me to just pick up and go on from here."

"I didn't do any of that to you, Mr. Haller. Please don't do this," begged Purser. "We just paid you to settle our case. Please don't hurt me anymore. I'll do anything you want."

"I want you to suffer," snarled Haller, turning all of the knobs to maximum power. Smoke rose from the clips. Purser cried out until his throat was hoarse and his lungs empty. Finally, Haller turned the power down, bringing Purser back to something akin to a normal state of consciousness.

"Now you know how my little girl felt when they poisoned her body with chemicals and shot her head with radiation," Haller growled through clenched teeth. "You know how it felt for her to deal with unimaginable pain." Haller walked around to the opposite side of the table as he spoke, never averting his stare from Purser's wide and horrified eyes.

"You're right, doctor. Killing you won't do a thing to undo my daughter's suffering, and it sure won't take away the pain my wife has felt every day since Jennifer died. Killing those other men didn't do that, either."

"What other men?" Purser asked.

"Bill Sellett, the lawyer you guys used to push through your tort reform package, and Senator Dunbar, who sponsored the bill. Did you know those men, doctor?"

"I have no idea who those people are," muttered Purser.

"They're the people who kept us from being able to get justice by suing you. And Lewis Cashman, up in New York, his insurance company wouldn't pay for Jennifer's surgery. So he had to pay himself."

As he told Purser of the other victims, Ed Haller felt a curious blend of satisfaction and sorrow. Purser's death wouldn't bring back his daughter, but the people responsible for his family's destruction had to be held accountable.

Haller thought of his service in the Middle East, where military operations took the lives of people rather than undoing damage already done. It was the price paid for enforcing a code of responsibility. Those military operations, though not personal retribution for him, had killed people by the hundreds and thousands, and had permanently altered the lives of families whose fathers and brothers wouldn't return from the urban battlefield.

For Haller and many like him in the military, the lives of victims and their families weren't the only lives changed. Depression among returning veterans ran rampant, most of it untreated. Post traumatic stress disorder, substance abuse, and suicide all occurred with higher frequency in veterans than in the general population, and veterans of the Middle East wars had the highest instance of all of these mental illnesses. Nearly a quarter of living veterans were homeless, compared to about eleven percent of the total population.

Haller felt all of this collective misery as he prepared to end the life of Dr. Robert Purser. Haller's military training had taught him to compartmentalize his feelings, to disregard the sorrow and guilt over the loss of human life and concentrate instead on fulfillment of the mission. Usually, his missions were chosen by others, civilians in office buildings far from harm's way. This time, he had chosen his own mission, and he alone had determined how it would be carried out.

True, he'd been put in this position because of his love for his family and his need to protect them. He hadn't protected Jennifer. He'd lost her because he was half a world away protecting others. Now, he had to protect Julie, and he couldn't fail this time. It would have been easy, even natural, to feel sorry for himself, but Ed Haller realized he had only himself to credit or to blame. As he stood peering down on his helpless victim, he found himself doing both.

# CHAPTER 45

Roaring toward Fort Worth, Grant dialed the cell number of T. Scott Wynn.

"Hello, Grant," Wynn said. "I didn't think I'd be hearing from you. Did we miss something in the settlement papers?"

"No, Scott, everything's fine with the settlement. That's all done. Have you talked to Dr. Purser today?"

"Why would I?" Wynn asked. "The case is over. We settled. In fact, I doubt he wants to talk to me. He's mad as hell that I recommended the settlement."

"Can you give him a call?" asked Grant. "Now, if you don't mind."

"What for?"

"Just trust me on this, Scott," Grant said, using all his willpower to control the tone of his voice. "I think Dr. Purser may be in danger. I can't explain, but this is no bullshit, Scott. I need you to call him. Now."

"You have to tell me more to get me to trust you, Grant," Wynn said. "Why don't you just tell me why you think he's in danger."

Grant knew it wasn't in Wynn's nature to trust another lawyer. "Let's do this, Scott," he said. "Please call him. I'm begging you. Call his office, his cell, and his home. If you find him, call me back

THE PRICE OF LIFE


and tell me I'm nuts. If you don't, call me back and tell me you couldn't reach him."

Wynn hesitated. "Sure, Grant. But you know how I love a good bottle of wine. If you're running me around, and I get Purser in the next ten minutes, you owe me a bottle of Insignia. And I want the '97."

"Make it a magnum, Scott. Just call him, and call me back when you find out something."

"What's in it for you if you win?" Wynn asked.

"I already won, remember?" Grant said. "I just hope I owe you that magnum."

Ten minutes stretched forever as Grant sped toward Weatherford. When his cell rang, he heard what he'd expected.

"You're off the hook," Wynn said.

"Did you reach anybody, or just voicemails?"

"I got his wife. She said he called her from the office almost two hours ago, saying he was on his way," Wynn said. "Now what the hell is going on?"

"I don't know exactly, Scott, but I swear I'll call you as soon as I know something."

Grant heard the faint tones of T. Scott Wynn swearing as he disconnected the call. He swerved through traffic, ignoring the horns of the drivers around him as he dialed the home number of Ed and Julie Haller. Julie picked up on the second ring.

"Julie, it's Grant Mercer."

"Hello, Grant," Julie chirped. "It's so good to hear from you."

"Is Ed there? I need to talk to him."

"No, Grant. Ed went to the gym, then he's going to meet a friend of his for a beer. He should be back in an hour or two, if you want me to have him call you."

"That's okay," Grant said, trying to keep his voice calm. "I'll call his cell."

"Is everything all right, Grant?" Julie asked.

"Everything's fine. I'll talk to you later."

Grant felt his heart pounding as he dialed the number. He'd noticed the look in his client's eyes, had sensed his desperation, but hadn't recognized just how desperate he was. Now, with the realization of what was happening descending upon him, Grant's blood ran cold.

Haller picked up on the fourth ring. "Good evening, Mr. Mercer." The voice was Haller's, but with a different tone. "So nice of you to call."

"Ed, can you take a few minutes and meet with me? We have something important to talk about."

"Actually, I'm a little busy," said Haller. "How about we meet in the morning? Maybe over breakfast." Grant thought he heard something strange when Haller spoke, but couldn't quite put his finger on it.

"Well, it's important, but I guess it'll wait until tomorrow," said Grant. "Where are you, anyway?"

"I'm finishing up a workout, then heading over to meet a friend. Why?" asked Haller.

"Just curious," Grant said. "How about we meet at Central Market? They do a good breakfast there."

"Sure. Eight o'clock too early?"

"Eight it is," Grant said. "See you then."

Haller closed his phone and contemplated the newly unconscious Dr. Purser.

As soon as the call was finished, Grant dialed the number Barlow had given him at the café.

"Sheriff, this is Grant Mercer. We have a problem, and I think you might be able to help."

"What's going on, Grant?" Barlow asked.

"You remember telling me you had a theory that all three cases were connected? I think you're right."

"Good, Grant. Let's get together tomorrow and talk about it."

"I think there may be one more, sheriff. We might have a chance to stop it, but I'll need your help."

Barlow stopped eating his meatloaf. "Go on, Grant."

"You remember me telling you about a case I had involving Castle Guard Insurance?" Grant started. "It's a medical malpractice case we just settled. My client in that case is a Marine. His name's Haller. He lost a leg in Tikrit about a year and a half ago, then lost his daughter to a brain tumor a couple months after that. I sued a doctor named Purser, the neurologist who missed the tumor. We just settled that case for two-fifty, and my client was understandably upset that we couldn't get any more."

"Get to the point, Grant," Barlow urged. "You said we might be able to prevent another murder."

"Sheriff, all three of your victims had some sort of connection to my client. Dunbar was the med mal reform sponsor and Sellett was the political muscle behind the scenes. What you probably don't know, and what I'd forgotten about until I read that newspaper article, is that Castle Guard Insurance, where this Cashman fellow was the CEO, denied coverage for Haller's little girl to have experimental surgery that might have saved her life."

"I'll be damned," Barlow said. "You think Haller killed all three?"

"I don't know for sure whether it would have made a difference," replied Grant, ignoring the question. "The doctor's failure to diagnose the tumor earlier probably doomed his daughter, but I doubt Haller sees it so clearly. I'm telling you, sheriff, the man's been through too much. He doesn't look like it on the outside, but inside he's broken. And I don't think he believes Dr. Purser got the punishment he deserved."

"What about the doctor? Where is he now?" asked Barlow.

"That's just it. I had his lawyer try to contact him a few minutes ago. No luck. Not at home, not at the office, not answering his cell."

"Lots of people ignore their cell phones, especially if they know it's a lawyer calling," Barlow said.

Grant recognized the barb, but didn't bite. "Look, sheriff, I know this seems thin, but ask yourself a question. If I didn't believe this was serious, would I be calling you, a cop, about my own client?"

"I don't know. Would you?"

"No," said Grant. "I talked to his wife a little while ago, then to him. His wife said he was at the gym, then going to meet a friend for a beer. He told me the same thing."

"Which gym?" asked Barlow.

"I don't think he's at the gym," said Grant. "When I talked to him, there was no noise in the background. You know how those places are these days, with the constant techno beat and hip hop music going all the time. I heard none of that, and none of the other gym noises, either. No people talking, no announcements, no weight machines or basketballs thumping."

"That doesn't mean he's got the doc."

"I know," Grant said. "But I also heard something else. His voice didn't sound the same."

"What do you mean?" Barlow asked.

"It just sounded like something was missing inside him. Everybody has a breaking point, Ronnie Clyde. I think my client has reached his."

"Tell you what, Grant. I'll call my amigo over at the FBI in Fort Worth. Then I need you to help us with something."

"Anything you need."

"You said you talked to Haller recently?"

"About five minutes ago," Grant confirmed.

"Give me the cell number."

Grant complied. "Are you going to call him?"

"No, sir," Barlow said. "You are. I need you to wait a few, then when I call you back with the go-ahead, I need you to call Haller and keep him on the phone. Don't spook him. Wherever he is, we need him to stay there for a few minutes, with you on the phone. I need at least three minutes, but four would be better. You think you can do that for us?"

"I don't know," Grant said. "When I talked to him, I told him I needed to see him. We set up a breakfast meeting for tomorrow. He might wonder why I'm calling back so soon."

"Tell him you talked to your wife and she's got you busy already. It doesn't matter what. A doctor's appointment or something at your kid's school. Just make up some shit that sounds plausible. You can do that, can't you counselor?" Barlow delivered the second lawyer jab in as many minutes.

"Sure I can," said Grant. "I make shit up for a living, remember?"

Barlow chuckled. "If you can keep him on the line for a few minutes, we can get a fix on his position based on his cell signal. We'll see where he is, and see if there's trouble for real. You'll need to keep in touch with Special Agent Will Thompson in Fort Worth. I'll give him a shout and vouch for you. We'll get back to you when they're ready to roll at the FBI office. You understand?"

"Okay, sheriff," said Grant. "I'll wait for your call."

Thompson was next to call, explaining to Grant the process of gaining the cooperation of Haller's cell phone provider and promising another call soon.

For the next five minutes Grant ran through a few scenarios about the lies he would tell Haller about the need for a meeting with him. Grant was troubled at the thought of setting up a client. Under ordinary circumstances, to betray a client's trust would be grounds for a grievance against a lawyer, perhaps for disbarment. But there are exceptions in cases in which the client plans to commit a crime or where harm might come to other people, and Grant knew it had to be done to save the life of Dr. Robert Purser.

As he recalled the details of the other murder cases from his discussion with Sheriff Barlow, he became more convinced than ever that Ed Haller had killed all three. Grant was deeply saddened by the thought of Haller committing such violence, and by the thought of the fate that surely awaited the Marine war veteran. For the moment, however, he had to do whatever he could to keep another man alive.

# CHAPTER 46

The call came from Barlow, and Grant redialed Ed Haller's cell number with shaky hands. The nighttime skyline of Fort Worth rose on the horizon, approaching fast as Grant weaved in and out of traffic.

"Sorry to call back so soon, Ed, but I can't make breakfast tomorrow after all. Wife has me down for the dentist. Says I cancelled the last two and have to go this time."

"Okay, Mr. Mercer," Haller said. "When do you want to meet?" Again, Grant heard an eerie quality to Haller's voice.

"I'd rather meet tonight, but I know you're busy." Grant struggled to quiet the tremble in his voice. "I thought I'd be available in the morning, but I have the dentist's appointment and a hearing after that."

"What about lunch tomorrow?"

"I'm tied up then, too." Grant stalled. "I don't know when we'll get the time."

"What's this all about, Mr. Mercer?" asked Haller.

Grant thought Haller would be getting irritated by now, but his voice gave away nothing, just the same hollow sound and feel Grant had picked up on before. "I think it would be best to do this in person. But now it looks like we may not get that chance anytime soon. It's about your settlement, Ed. I need to be sure you understand the potential tax consequences of the money."

"I thought you said there would be none."

"I said I didn't think so, but I wanted you to talk to a CPA to be sure." Grant looked at his watch. Barely a minute had passed.

"That's right, you did tell us. Is that what this is all about? That doesn't sound like a big deal."

"Uh, that was only one thing," Grant stammered. "I thought we should also get together about investment of the money. I know you might have somebody in mind, but I can refer you to a fellow who's taken care of several of my clients over the years. They've all been pleased with his work. I'll go with you and Julie, if you like."

"Mr. Mercer, I already told you I have somebody to handle the money. It's not like there was a lot of it anyway, but we've already taken care of that. Now what are you calling about?"

Grant had only burned a couple of minutes, and knew he needed more. "Here's the deal, Ed. I got a bill yesterday from one of our experts for another eight thousand bucks. I didn't know he'd send it, so I didn't include it in my expense listing. Of course, we've already distributed the money, and I need to talk to you about getting reimbursed for that bill." Grant hoped this would at least generate some conversation.

Haller let out a sigh. "I know you need to recover your costs and all, but it seems like it was your responsibility to account for that stuff. I'll be happy to talk to you about that whenever you can make time, but not tonight."

"Thanks, Ed." Grant needed a few more seconds. "This is really embarrassing. It doesn't happen very often. I sure would appreciate talking to you about that. I know it was my responsibility, and not your fault, but my partners are mighty chapped and, well, it would probably come right out of my own pocket. When can we get together?"

"Like I said, anytime," said Haller. "Just tell me when."

"Anytime in particular sound good?" asked Grant, fairly sure he'd spent enough time by now.

"Wednesday of next week. Lunch. Mi Cocina on the west side," said Haller.

"Good," said Grant. "See you then."

Haller was already gone.

# CHAPTER 47

While Grant kept Haller on the line, Special Agent Thompson directed traffic from the Fort Worth field office. After a brief discussion with Sheriff Barlow, he'd spent a furious fifteen minutes getting orders for Haller's cell phone to be monitored.

A few years before, the federal government issued an edict that all cell phone service providers upgrade their systems to provide more exact locations of the phones on their network by using Global Positioning Satellite technology. The obsolete triangulation method depended on equipment on each cell tower gauging relative position based on the strength of the signals sent between the telephone and the towers. The timing of these signals could be used to calculate the distance from the towers to the phone. Because it's left to interpretation of these calculations to determine the location of the phone, triangulation is relatively inaccurate.

In the case of a GPS system, a chip installed in the telephone continuously assesses and reports the position of the telephone with the assistance of information beamed to it via an array of satellites in orbit about the earth. These telephones make it possible to determine location with extreme accuracy.

Thompson had hoped Haller's phone would be the GPS variety. It turned out to be without such a chip, which would further complicate matters. The telephone company originally balked at cooperating with the FBI to determine the location of Haller's cell phone.

Thompson was amazed, thinking the company was surely familiar with the regulations by now, including those requiring cooperation with Public Safety Answering Points, which included the FBI field offices around the country. True, the regulations required cooperation upon proper request by the law enforcement people, but there wasn't time for a warrant. Only a call from the deputy director to the vice president of the phone company finally secured the cell phone provider's full cooperation. Even so, it would be impossible to determine Haller's exact location.

Grant Mercer's cell number appeared on the screen of Thompson's phone. "Got him," Thompson said without a greeting. "He's just east of Weatherford, about two miles south of the interstate down Trinity Road. You know where that is?"

"Damn," said Grant. "I just left Weatherford."

"He has a regular phone, no GPS, so I don't know exactly where he is. Best we can do is a grid of about four blocks. I'm sending the Weatherford PD and the Parker County Sheriff, along with Sheriff Barlow," said Thompson. "I'm coming right behind them with another half dozen agents."

"Nobody else can get there for another thirty minutes at least," said Grant. "What do I do until then?"

"Stay in touch with me and Barlow. Look around and tell us what you find. If you spot Haller, don't go in yourself," said Thompson. "Wait for the cavalry."

"I'm not crazy," Grant said. "Besides, you said it's only good for about four blocks. How will I know exactly where he is? There's no way we can find him quickly."

"That's right," Thompson said. So don't think you have to try to be the hero. Just see what you can see and keep me in the loop. I'm on my way now."

# CHAPTER 48

Grant took the first ramp off the freeway, ran the red light, and screamed back down the on-ramp headed west. The Tahoe took him to his exit in Weatherford in five minutes, and he turned down Trinity Road. A mile south of the freeway stood a group of buildings barely visible in the yellow glow of the lights mounted on poles in the parking lots. Forty warehouse and office spaces occupied four large structures, all clustered toward the center of the tract of land on which they sat. Around the perimeter of each building were doors of varying sizes and designs, from access doors for people to overhead and swinging doors large enough to accommodate trucks and their cargo.

Grant picked the building closest to him and parked his car around the corner, fifty feet from the nearest door. He set his cell phone to vibrate and stuffed it into his back pocket. As he stepped toward the building, it occurred to him how ridiculous this scene was, and how right Thompson had been to tell him to stay put. He had no weapon, no flashlight, and most of all no training in how to handle a situation like this.

Haller was somewhere in one of these buildings, probably armed and certainly trained to handle himself in combat. Grant knew he might be too late, and might not find Haller at all. Even if he did, he'd likely be unable to stop any crime in progress. Another fifteen minutes of waiting on the professionals might cost Purser his life, so he pressed ahead.

Grant's eyes adjusted slowly to the darkness. Shadows cut slanting lines across the cracked asphalt parking lot, cast by vapor lights at the corners of the warehouses. Walking down the side of the first building, he saw nothing out of the ordinary. It was nearly eight o'clock and the place was essentially abandoned. A few cars and trucks remained, but he saw no activity anywhere in the lot or around the buildings.

Turning the corner, Grant saw light coming from a small window in the front door of one of the warehouse spaces. A sign above the door, lit with floodlights mounted on curved metal supports, read *Carter's Custom Choppers* and bore a Gothic logo amidst skulls and other exotic artwork.

Grant crept to the edge of the door, peering through the window. He could see a couple of motorcycles in a state of semi-disassembly, but no noises emanated from within, and there was no sign of anyone present. He moved on, and found nothing else of interest in the first building.

He crossed another part of the parking lot to get to the next structure and saw that the second door from the right also had a light shining through its small window. There was no sign above the door, although a small *Silver Star Conversions* plaque hung on the wall. Grant moved carefully to the edge of the door, adjusting his head to a position where could see inside.

A small reception area was within, but there was no furniture at the moment. A half wall with a sliding glass partition separated the reception area from an office behind the glass. No desk was visible from Grant's vantage point, but through the open sliding glass window he could see an empty metal bookshelf positioned next to an open door leading to warehouse space behind. Grant had a clear view of the interior of the warehouse and the wall separating this space from the adjacent one, but could see nothing in the way of supplies or other materials.

Grant paused for a moment, thinking that something about the warehouse space didn't look right. Something about the quality of the lighting didn't quite fit. He would have expected fluorescent lighting, but the bright white light cast on the walls told him that some other sort of bulb, perhaps halogen or mercury vapor, illuminated the space.

As he chewed on this problem, the light in the office dimmed, as did the light in the garage. This was followed immediately by the unmistakable sound of a person screaming, which froze Grant in his tracks. Another scream followed as the lights dimmed again. This time, Grant didn't just freeze. He felt a sudden tightening in his stomach and was sure he would retch.

Grant blinked hard, fighting to regain his focus. A couple of deep breaths fended off the nausea, and he looked back through the window to see Ed Haller walk in front of the door, quickly turn around, and return to the garage.

Grant immediately ducked below the level of the window, hoping Haller hadn't seen him, and waited for what seemed like forever before peeking through the window again. Seeing nothing and nobody, he quickly stepped away from the door. As soon as he thought he was far enough away, he flipped open his cell and dialed Barlow.

"It's Grant," he whispered. "Where are you?"

"On my way, about five miles from Weatherford. Where are you?"

"Trinity Road Industrial Park. You know the place?"

"Nope," Barlow said, "but I got the area from Thompson based on the cell signal."

"Come down Trinity, about a mile south of the interstate. You can't miss it. Only industrial park around. Right side of the road. I'm at building E, on the north side. And Sheriff Barlow?"

"Yes?"

"Haller's here. I just saw him."

Barlow swore. "Anybody with him?"

"Not that I can see, but I did hear a man screaming."

"Okay, then," said Barlow. "Stay there. Don't do anything stupid. The feds will be there in about twenty minutes, and the local guys sooner than that."

"Better hurry." Grant jammed the phone back into his pocket.

Staying low, he crawled back to the doorway, pressing closely to the rough concrete wall and catching his breath. He leaned left, looking through the glass door, scanning the small space without seeing any activity

Grant felt a cold, hard circle on the back of his head, then heard the click of an automatic handgun being cocked.

"Good evening, Mr. Mercer," Haller said graciously. "How nice of you to join us."

# CHAPTER 49

Grant gulped hard, trying to stay calm. "Ed, listen to me."

"Quiet down, counselor," said Haller. "Let's go inside." The empty, disinterested tone Grant had heard on the phone was gone, replaced by the sound of a man completely focused on the job at hand.

"Okay, Ed," Grant labored to keep his voice steady and his bowels under control. "I'm on your side. Just take it easy."

Haller's left hand held the collar and left shoulder of Grant's jacket as the right pressed the barrel of the military issue nine-millimeter Beretta semi-automatic pistol into the lowest part of the back of Grant's skull. He'd always been amazed at the strength of Haller's handshake. Grant now knew Haller's left hand was just as powerful as the right, and it wasn't a pleasant thought.

Haller steered Grant past the closed overhead door, around the corner of the building, and up to a windowless metal door, which Grant opened at Haller's command. The two men stepped through the door and into a world which Grant scarcely knew existed.

Two sets of intensely bright halogen bulbs were attached to metal stands, shining blinding light into the corner of the warehouse bay where a cart held what looked to be surgical equipment. A table propped to a slight angle held a naked Dr. Robert Purser in leather straps by the waist, chest, legs, and arms. Purser had small metal objects attached to his chest, neck, ears, and groin. It took Grant a few seconds to notice the small wires leading from each of these objects and realize they were electrodes.

Grant saw a tattered chunk of flesh missing from Purser's left ribcage. Purser bled from small wounds scattered about his chest, neck, and groin. Not much blood, but each cut produced a red stream pointing toward the doctor's feet, sliding toward the outside of his body and out of sight. The left side of his neck glowed bright red, bloody from the resection of his earlobe on that side.

Purser's face was nothing short of a horror mask. Even without cuts or other wounds, it bore beyond a doubt the most gruesome expression Grant had ever seen. Cracked and bleeding lips drew back, exposing a twisted, agonizing grin. Purser's mouth fell silently open and moved in a random fashion, uttering a wordless plea. In Purser's eyes Grant saw raw, stark terror so profound they looked nearly inhuman. Grant tried to give Purser a reassuring look, fearing Haller would retaliate against any effort to speak, but nothing in Purser's expression led Grant to believe the message had been received.

"Have a seat," Haller said, shoving Grant toward a metal folding chair in the center of the room.

Grant did as he was told, and the two men looked at each other for a long moment. "Can we talk?" he asked Haller.

"Sure, counselor," said Haller, pointing the Beretta at his lawyer's chest. "We can talk. What do you want to talk about?"

"Don't do this, Ed. This is not who you are."

"How the hell do you know who I am?" demanded Haller. "Do you have any idea what I did for the Marines in Iraq?"

"I know you fought for your country. You're a hero."

"I'm no hero," screamed Haller, lunging toward Grant. "Heroes don't do the shit I had to do, what my Marines had to do.

Heroes protect people. When they fight, they fight for the right reasons, and they fight fair. We didn't do any of that."

Grant drew a breath, but stopped short of speaking when Haller looked his way again.

"Let me tell you what I was doing over there while you were busy suing people over here, counselor." The last word was spat out, like a bite of rotten fruit. "I was in intelligence for two tours. That means I had to get information about what was going on over there. And I had to get it by any means necessary. You understand what I mean by that?"

Grant felt a vibration in his hip pocket, his cell phone buzzing with an incoming call. A furtive glance at Haller told him that the buzz couldn't be heard. Grant nodded.

"This is all right out of the handbook." Haller swept a hand toward Dr. Purser and the table holding him tight. "They have drawings of it and everything, just so no dumb-ass leatherneck can fuck it up. Which instrument to use when, what voltage to use to keep a prisoner talking without passing out, the whole thing. I did thirty-four of these in twenty-six months. Three were women. Two were kids. One was only fourteen. He was the toughest son of a bitch of the bunch. Never got a fucking thing from him. Stab wounds, electric shock, acid, it didn't matter. Nothing fazed that boy. He toughed it out until he died." As he spoke, Haller's voice remained steady, but his eyes misted, and he looked over Grant's shoulder instead of his habitual direct eye contact.

"So you see, counselor," Haller hissed, "this is exactly who I am."

"We're not in Iraq, Ed," Grant said. "And this man isn't the enemy."

"Sure he is." Haller shot an icy glare at Grant. "He took my little girl from me."

"We did what we could do about that," Grant said. "You hired me, and we did what we had to do to stand up for Jennifer. You told me that's what you wanted to do, to stand up for her."

"Is that really what we did?" Haller said, more to himself than to Grant. "How can that be? We got $250,000 for my daughter's life. Is that what she's worth? The cost of a nice house? A nice big boat for one of those insurance company assholes? Prize money on some game show? Was my daughter really worth just two-fifty?"

"No, Ed, she was worth so much more. Children are priceless. Mine, yours, and everyone else's." It was all Grant knew to say.

"You told me that before," muttered Haller. Sadness dripped from his voice like wax, and tears now ran down both cheeks. Haller made no move to wipe them away. "So why do they get away with it? Why do they all get away with it?

"Over in the Middle East, we've sacrificed thousands of soldiers so Halliburton and Schlumberger can rebuild oil refineries and power plants. Hell, the Air Force blows shit up over there and bulldozers clear off the rubble for new construction before the smoke clears.

"On top of the dead ones, we got people coming back with parts missing, like me." Haller pointed at his leg. "Only when we get here, they tell us we're not covered for all the care we need. They tell us we can see the folks in San Antonio, but if they can't help us, there's nothing more they can do. We've got it pretty good, the guys who lost arms and legs. At least we can get some help.

"Just about everybody who's been there is screwed up in the head. You watch guys getting killed, you see kids stumbling out of a building we just bombed, their skin still burning, crying and looking for their mother. You do shit like this to people you don't even know." Ed gestured again toward Purser, who looked as though he heard Haller's diatribe, but couldn't understand. "I once went thirteen days with no sleep. I was too damn scared of the nightmares to close my eyes.

"I know guys who were in the strike zone of some of the bombings, down there holding lasers so the bombs could hit their targets. The guys who came back are shooting fire. Their semen's toxic. They either can't have kids or their babies are born with birth defects. Our government tells them there's no proof that anything in the war caused the problem. Besides, they've separated from the service, and the kids aren't on the military's insurance plan." Haller let out an evil, sardonic laugh.

"There's another great example. Castle Guard Insurance. The premiums from the military coverage alone totaled more than ten billion dollars last year. Ten billion. But when it comes time to cover surgery for somebody's daughter, they say it's experimental, and they don't cover it.

"All that adds up, counselor. It makes you crazy. When we come home, the military tells us we're through. 'Just go on ahead with your civilian life,' they say. Well, it's not that simple, Mr. Mercer. When they train you to kill, it's tough adjusting to a world where killing is frowned upon.

"Then when my little girl died," continued Haller, his voice cracking and his eyes streaming tears, "I found out they've fixed that up nice for themselves, too. Even with a fine lawyer like you, Mr. Mercer, the best we can do is a lousy two-fifty."

"You're right, Ed," Grant said, conscious that Haller still held the gun in his hand, still pointing it directly at Grant's chest. "The whole thing sucks. But man, we have to figure out a way to put a stop to it. You have to think about Julie and Bradley. What'll your wife and son do?"

"We're way past that, counselor." Haller moved carefully toward Purser and the table, gun still aimed at Grant. He reached to the cart at the side of the table, put down the pistol, and chose a syringe. "Stay there, Mr. Mercer."

Haller raised the needle to eye level, depressing the plunger and flicking at the side of the plastic tube to see that no air remained. He looked casually at Purser and injected five hundred milligrams of Phenobarbital. As Haller set the syringe down and picked up the weapon, Purser's eyes fell shut.

"That should keep him out for awhile," mumbled Haller. He picked up the pistol and walked back toward Grant, stopping in front of the chair. "It's just you and me now, Mr. Mercer. Just a man and his lawyer. You want to talk?"

"Absolutely, Ed. Let's talk."

Haller exhaled. "Julie looked into this when we first started talking about a lawsuit. When you told us about the damage cap, I told her we should just forget it. We both realized we'd never be able to get a fair shake in the courts. I didn't want to hire you, but Julie insisted. She kept saying the people responsible for Jennifer had to pay."

Grant's mind spun, trying to make sense of what Haller was telling him and why. He was tempted to interrupt, to tell Haller he already knew about the first three crimes. Instead, he stayed quiet.

"Julie showed me all the research she did. You'd be proud of that part, Mr. Mercer. She had articles about that state senator pushing tort reform. I didn't pay much attention when she did that. Then she showed me some stuff about Sellett, the lobbyist. She said he was the real force behind the law. She said he's the one who's letting Dr. Purser off Scot-free." Haller jerked a thumb over his shoulder toward his comatose victim.

"I told her to leave it alone. I said that's why we had you. I knew you'd do a good job for us. She just kept repeating herself--these people have to pay."

Grant tilted his head up slightly, watching Ed Haller shake his head slowly while telling his story. In that instant, Grant understood, and knew he'd been wrong.

Haller saw the realization on his lawyer's face. "I should have seen it coming. When I saw Sellett had been killed, it didn't really register. But when the guy in New York went down, I put it together and confronted Julie. She didn't have to admit what she'd done. I knew she'd killed those men before she said a word."

Grant's heart sank. "Don't say anymore, Ed. Please just be quiet."

"I know this is privileged, counselor. There's nothing you can do. You still represent Julie and me, so you can't tell anyone about this. Even if you did, no prosecutor can use it."

"That doesn't make it right," Grant said. He was dizzy again, his mind overwhelmed by fear, anger, and sadness.

"Probably not," Said Haller. "But I know one thing. That senator and the lawyer from Austin were probably pretty happy about getting their law passed. I bet they had a big party for all their doctor buddies and their insurance clients. Well, they're not happy now, are they, counselor? And that smug bastard in New York figured his company would save millions of dollars by denying surgery for Jennifer. That wound up costing him big-time, too.

"I didn't figure out what Julie was doing until it was too late. She always had a cover. She left Bradley with her parents and had excuses to be out of town. She actually came with me to Washington for that military conference, but told me she didn't want to go to New York for the depositions. She went up on a flight before me, killed Mr. Cashman, and got back to Texas before I did.

"So you see, Mr. Mercer, it's too late now. Julie already killed those other three men. But everybody thinks I did it. I know the cops are on their way, and they can wrap it up all nice and neat when they have me. I can't let my wife go to prison for the rest of her life. This one's on me. What difference will it make if I let Purser live? Will they let me go because I took pity on him?"

"I guess not." Grant shook his head slowly. He tried to process all this information and figure out the legal ramifications. Unfortunately, most of his knowledge was from the criminal law class he took in law school more than twenty years before. "Ed, I'm not a criminal lawyer and I don't know how all that works. But I know that if you let Dr. Purser live, and let me help you, that story ends much better than the one where Dr. Purser dies. Don't you see that?"

"Don't you see, Mr. Mercer?" said Haller, "Dr. Purser has to die. He's the last one who hurt Jennifer. If I let him go, I let my daughter down."

"He hurt her, all right," said Grant, shifting uneasily in his chair. "But he didn't mean to. He wanted to help Jennifer. He made a mistake."

Haller turned toward the doctor, eyeing his unconscious captive curiously. "We've already talked about that, he and I have. Maybe he didn't mean to hurt her, but he did. He killed her. And his life hasn't changed a bit since then. His insurance company paid to settle the case. He's still playing golf a couple times a week and still driving a Bentley. Besides, if I don't kill him, Julie will. They'll start up the investigation again, and she'll eventually get caught. I can't let that happen."

# CHAPTER 50

Special Agent Thompson and four of his colleagues approached as silently as possible from the east side of the building. Sheriff Barlow led a team of five tactical officers from the Weatherford Police Department from the west. Thompson was first to arrive at the front door of the warehouse space. He looked through the window and saw the back of Ed Haller. He could hear voices coming from inside, but couldn't understand the conversation.

Thompson signaled Barlow and his men to stay put, trying to decide quickly what to do. Grant hadn't answered his cell phone, and since they hadn't seen the lawyer when they arrived in the industrial park, Thompson assumed he was inside, along with Haller and Purser. That meant there were two innocents, potential victims, in the room with the suspect, which severely limited his options. The only other entrance to the warehouse, other than the door to the office, didn't present a viable alternative. It would be best if they could enter the office undetected, before they stormed the warehouse. Thompson estimated their chances of resolving the situation without loss of life at about ten percent. He hoped they could avoid losing more than one.

As Thompson mulled over his options, he heard Haller's voice rising. He was still unable to understand what was being said, but the

GREG McCARTHY

tone of voice sent a chill down Thompson's spine. He didn't have much time.

Thompson motioned for Barlow to come toward the door and crouched close to the ground to keep out of view through the glass. Barlow leaned closer, so the two men could converse in a whisper.

"We can't wait, sheriff," said Thompson. "You hear that man's voice?"

Barlow clenched his jaw. "What's the plan?"

"He's alone, right?"

Barlow nodded his agreement.

"Then let's just make it you and me. Maybe if he just sees a couple of us, it'll keep him from freaking out. Maybe we can get him calm and keep from having to shoot anybody."

"Good plan," said Barlow. "How do you intend do that? If Mercer's in there with him, he's bound to know we've put him on three murders. He's got nothing to lose."

Thompson paused a moment. "This is our only chance. And we have to move now."

Barlow nodded again. "Let's do it."

The two of them returned to their respective teams and advised the men of the plan. The others would wait outside the door, firearms at the ready, while Barlow and Thompson entered the warehouse space with their guns holstered. Each man wore a flak vest under his shirt, but they provided no protection from shots to the head.

Barlow arrived at the door first. The unspoken agreement was that he would be the first into the room, as well as the primary spokesman for the pair. He put his hand on the door handle and, with a nod to Thompson, slowly swung the door inward. The voices inside the garage bay stopped, and Barlow crouched at the edge of the open doorway leading from the office into the bay.

# CHAPTER 51

Grant watched the door swing open.

"Captain Haller," Barlow announced in a firm, authoritative voice, "I'm Sheriff Ronnie Barlow. I'd like to talk for a few minutes. That all right with you?"

"Go away, sheriff." Haller's voice was calm. "We're fine here."

"I need to talk to you, Captain. I have my weapon holstered, and I don't want to use it. I mean you no harm." Barlow cast a glance at Thompson, still out of Haller's line of sight. "I have a friend with me. We're coming into the garage."

Barlow stepped carefully around the corner, hands at shoulder level. Ed Haller stood in the middle of the room, pointing a gun at the doorway. Thompson came through the entrance and saw Haller, with Grant Mercer in a chair about five feet away and obviously relieved that he no longer had a pistol aimed at him. Purser remained strapped to the gurney in the corner, naked and bleeding from several small wounds, still unconscious.

"Hello, Captain," said Thompson, stepping into the bay behind Barlow and stopping alongside the sheriff, his hands also raised to his shoulders. "I'm Will Thompson. I'm a friend of Sheriff Barlow. I hope we can talk about this."

"Nothing to talk about, Mr. Thompson. I told you, we're all fine here," said Haller. "You fellows shouldn't have come."

It was Barlow's turn. "Grant, you okay?"

"Yeah," said Grant, "thanks for asking. We're all right. I was just talking with my client."

"Tell you what, gentlemen," said Barlow. "Why don't we get Dr. Purser to the hospital so he can get him some help? Will and Grant and I will go with you, Captain Haller, and talk about what's happened, see if we can figure out how everyone can come out of this okay."

"No way to come out okay," said Haller, his voice rising a half octave, the cadence of his speech quickening. "Too much shit already happened."

"Put the gun down, Ed," Grant said. "Mr. Thompson and the sheriff will help, won't you, guys?"

"Sure," Barlow said as Thompson nodded. "We'll do everything we can for you and your family. Please believe me, Captain. You've served your country. You've made great sacrifices. We appreciate all you've done. We'll do all we can to help. You have my word on that." Barlow's voice stayed calm, his eyes riveted on Haller.

"Think, Ed," Grant pleaded. The dizzying revelations made it hard for Grant to do what he was asking of Haller. "Think about Julie. Think about Bradley. You have to think about them."

Haller slowly turned his gaze toward Purser. After a long silence spent studying his subject, he turned back to Grant. Haller's eyes bore a different look than they had just moments before. They were softer, and certainly less frightening. Grant believed for the first time the situation could be resolved without anyone else dying.

"You're right," Haller said. "I have to think about my family."

Haller swung his pistol away from Barlow and Thompson, and again pointed it directly at Grant. Barlow tensed, slowly bringing his right hand to the holster he wore on his right hip, reaching for the handle of his revolver there. Thompson did the same. Haller's face changed expression to a disturbing look of uneasy resignation.

"Ed, please," Grant begged. "Think about your family. Hell, think about mine. You're a good man. Don't do this."

"Thank you, Mr. Mercer," said Haller, his voice quivering. "I appreciate your kind words. Yours, too, sheriff. I expect you to keep your word about helping my family."

"Absolutely," said Barlow. "Just put the gun down, and we can talk."

Barlow carefully slipped the revolver about halfway out of its holster, his index finger against the trigger guard. Thompson was in a similar position three feet away.

Haller looked briefly at Barlow and Thompson, then looked back at Grant, a distressed smile crossing his face. As he lowered his gun, he said, "Will you see to it they keep their word, Mr. Mercer?"

"You bet," answered Grant. "Just like he said."

"Thank you."

Suddenly, Haller swung his arm upward, grasping the butt of the pistol with both hands and aiming it directly at Grant. At the same time, his feet spread apart, knees bending to provide a solid base for the discharge of the weapon. It was a move that could only be perceived as aggression by the two lawmen. They drew their guns simultaneously, bringing their pistol hands up and aiming their weapons directly at Ed Haller in one swift and synchronized motion.

Haller's face relaxed as he pointed the gun at Grant and cocked the hammer. While Thompson and Barlow brought their weapons to bear, Haller had a clear shot at Grant, and enough time to squeeze off three rounds, maybe four. Instead, he looked directly at Grant and gave a slight nod.

Barlow and Thompson, of course, weren't focused on Haller's face, but instead on his posture and the simple fact that he was about to shoot Grant Mercer. Grant recognized too late what Haller was doing, screaming for Barlow and Thompson not to shoot. He couldn't blame them for thinking his plea was directed at Haller.

Barlow's Colt Python .357 Magnum and Thompson's Beretta discharged within milliseconds of one another. Barlow was a good shot and had more experience on the range than Thompson, but the FBI agent's superior firearm simply processed the projectiles more efficiently, ejecting spent cartridges faster than Barlow's Colt could turn the chamber to have the next bullet ready to fire. As a result, Thompson fired four shots and Barlow only two. The difference in the performance of the pistols hardly mattered.

The first slug from Thompson tore into Haller's right shoulder, shattering the humerus about three inches below the joint and causing Haller to drop his gun. The first shot was immediately followed by another entering through the right side of his abdomen and exiting through his back. This second bullet missed all organs and was essentially a flesh wound. Barlow's first shot was fired too quickly, and hit Haller in the prosthetic leg, ricocheting into the sheetrock wall of the office and producing a sharp, metallic ping. The second struck Haller in the chest, entering between the third and fourth rib and lodging just inside his left shoulder blade.

Meanwhile, two more shots from Thompson found their mark, both hammering into Haller's chest within inches of each other, breaking the ribs they struck and passing through his left lung. One slug tore a gaping hole in the pulmonary vein, and Haller's rapid heart rate quickly pumped an enormous quantity of blood into his chest cavity. As Haller dropped to his knees, bright pink foam sprayed from his mouth and nose. His pained, ghoulish grimace was now heavily tinted red as he slumped to the floor.

Grant quickly moved forward, kicking Haller's gun out of the way and kneeling next to his wounded client.

"Couldn't let you take the fall for me, counselor," Haller gasped, choking on the blood bubbling in his throat.

"Don't talk, Ed," said Grant. "Guys, do we have an ambulance on the way?"

"Two of them," Barlow said. "They should be here any minute." Barlow holstered his weapon and reached for his cell phone, anxious for medical help to arrive as soon as possible.

"Grant," said Haller, his voice hoarse and weak, "look after my wife and son. Tell them I love them." He choked and coughed. "Remember what I told you. It had to be this way."

"Sure thing," said Grant, his shirt now covered with a fine mist of blood, the result of Haller gagging and spitting as he tried to converse. He held Ed Haller's shoulder with one hand and his head with the other. Grant watched the life drain from Haller's eyes and witnessed a soldier's last breath.

He looked at Purser, then at Barlow and Thompson, who stood still and silent a few feet away. Grant held the head of his dead client, pulled Haller close to his chest, and lost the fight to hold back his tears.

# CHAPTER 52

One week later, Grant and Samantha Mercer attended the funeral of Captain Ed Haller, United States Marine Corps. Haller was buried in his dress blues, but without military honors. With all evidence pointing to Haller as the perpetrator of three homicides and a brutal torture session, the Defense Department determined it wasn't in the best interest of the nation to have a full military funeral for a triple murderer.

Fortunately, the Pentagon had decided Haller's family wouldn't lose any benefits that would otherwise have been theirs. This decision was influenced in no small measure by Colonel Marcus Hanson, the Marine officer who tried valiantly, though in vain, to help Julie Haller in her quest to have Castle Guard Insurance pay for Jennifer's laser surgery. Hanson hadn't needed much persuasion, but had taken several calls from Grant, who'd been determined to be a pest if necessary.

The Mercers sat with the Haller family, Julie seated immediately to Grant's right, throughout the funeral and memorial service. Most of Haller's closest friends were in the military and on active duty in the Middle East, so it fell to Grant to deliver the eulogy. It was, beyond any doubt, the most difficult speech he'd ever made.

Scarcely able to keep his voice under control, Grant was sincere if not exactly eloquent. He choked back tears as he praised

Haller as a devoted family man and war hero. He described Haller's love for his son and daughter, and fought through an emotional five minutes about Haller's courage in recovering from the effects of his military service, both mental and physical. For much different reasons, he found it nearly impossible to get through his remarks about the effects of the family's travails on Haller's widow.

When he finished, Grant sat next to Julie Haller to listen to the remainder of the service. He resisted the urge to look at her, afraid of what she might see in him, but more frightened of what he might see in the eyes of such an unlikely killer.

He'd depended on Samantha to go to the Haller home on the night of the shooting, along with Sheriff Barlow, and had managed not to see Julie in person since then. His telephone conversations with her had been short and without any small talk.

Since Haller's revelations about his wife's rampage, Grant had wrestled with the question of how to handle the information. He knew he would probably lose his license if he revealed what he knew to the police, and no court would allow any information gained from the disclosure to be used in trial.

He considered dropping hints to Sheriff Barlow so he could stay out of the picture while Barlow and the FBI re-started the investigation. This sounded plausible, but Grant realized that, even if he maintained his license, Julie Haller would go to prison. This wouldn't bring back Ed Haller, or Jennifer, or the victims of Julie's rage. It would, however, leave Bradley Haller without his mother. The boy had already lost his sister and his father, and had just turned seven. It was already too much.

After the service, Grant walked across the cemetery to retrieve the Tahoe for the trip home. As he opened the door, he saw Julie Haller standing at the back of the truck. Her hair fell gently in golden waves across her shoulders, barely resting on the fabric of her simple black dress. The string of pearls around her neck provided the only adornment, save for her wedding and engagement rings, still on the third finger of her left hand. She removed her black sunglasses and smiled warmly.

"Thank you for a lovely eulogy, Grant."

"You're welcome," he said as he looked away, searching for the Tahoe and wondering how to walk away without further discussion.

"Grant, look at me," Julie said. Grant turned painstakingly toward her. After a long pause, she said simply, "You know."

Grant drew a deep breath. "I just don't know what I'm supposed to do about that."

Julie flashed her most comely smile. "Nothing at all, Grant. The police can't use anything you tell them, and there's no sense in losing your law license. What's done is done. You should do nothing at all."

Grant's poker face never came to him, and the shock was plain. Julie's warm smile turned to a cruel grin, her eyes narrowing until the blue of her irises could barely be seen.

"Tell me, Grant, what did you really expect to happen? Are you going to tell me you think the money we got in our lawsuit is justice? Is that money supposed to make it right?"

"Of course not," replied Grant. "But God, Julie, this is something else completely. Those other men didn't do anything to you or your family."

"They didn't?" Julie sneered. "The man at Castle Guard took away the last chance I had to save my little girl. The other two wanted a system where nobody could get anything meaningful in the courts. They got what they wanted. I guess they figured everybody would just give up." She leaned closer, keeping her eyes on his. "Well, not me. I didn't give up. They got the system they wanted," she hissed. "People should be careful what they wish for, don't you think?"

"Do me a favor, Julie. Get some help." Grant couldn't believe this was the same client who seemed so pure, so vulnerable, and so innocent when they met. He took a long, slow step away from Julie Haller.

"I don't need any help for what happened to those men," she said softly. "And there's nothing that will help me for the loss of my daughter and my husband."

"Your husband took the bullet for you, Julie," Grant snarled, stepping closer. "He figured out what you did, and he wouldn't let you go down for it."

"That's what good men like Ed do, Grant," Julie said with a shrug. "They protect people. Ed did it all his life."

Grant stuffed his hands into his pockets and shook his head. "I should have figured it out before it got to that. Maybe I could have stopped you. Maybe I could have protected Ed."

"Don't flatter yourself, Grant," Julie said. "You're a good lawyer, but you're not that smart."

The insult stung, but her frosty delivery made him practically numb.

"What about Purser?" Grant asked. "He's still around. Don't tell me you weren't planning something for him, too."

"Purser's not a problem anymore," she said, her face brightening again into a wondrous smile. "He got what he had coming to him. He paid. They all paid."

"I can't withhold anything you tell me about committing a crime in the future. If you're planning anything with Purser, I can't protect you. And I won't"

"Why, Grant, I'm surprised," Julie said sweetly. "I wouldn't dream of such a thing." She stepped past him quickly. "Do take care, Mr. Mercer."

"Julie?" he said, looking over his shoulder as she walked away. When she stopped and turned, he came a bit closer, clearing his throat. He couldn't bring himself to look at her, and stared at his feet instead. "Ed loved you very much. You and Bradley and Jennifer. He wanted me to tell you."

"I already knew that, Grant." Julie turned and walked to the tent to join what remained of her family. Grant watched in disbelief, unable to move. Finally, when Julie Haller was out of sight, he trudged slowly away.

# EPILOGUE

Two weeks after Ed Haller's funeral, Grant met with his partner and told him of his intention to leave the firm. Charlie Montgomery was incredulous at first, but agreed that it was best for all concerned for Grant to exit, and sooner rather than later. Grant spent the next month working through the process of shifting authority on his cases from himself to Montgomery and the other lawyers in the firm and taking care of final details of the transition. The last few days he spent boxing up his personal belongings and finding a place to store his furniture.

Much of Grant's time, however, was spent contemplating the events of the Haller case. He slept little, and poorly when he did. He had a hard time purging his mind of the image of Julie Haller, lovely young wife and mother, savagely taking the lives of three men. Even more difficult was the thought of her mental condition, the damage done to her psyche that had driven her to acts she'd considered inconceivable just months before. Grant could understand it on one level, but couldn't shake the feeling of condemnation of his client for what she'd done.

Perhaps she'd been pushed too far, and felt understandably shortchanged about the lawsuit. Still, her vigilante justice was wrong, and Grant wondered how a person could do such an abrupt about-face. He remembered the look in Julie's eyes during their last conversation and wondered how her heart could be so hard. On the afternoon of Ed Haller's funeral, Grant had looked through Julie's eyes and into her soul. He had seen only darkness.

Grant's troubles were compounded by the fact that he couldn't discuss them with anyone. His partner was out of the question, as was his trusted friend Chris Turner, because he couldn't divulge privileged conversations. He couldn't talk to Samantha, who constantly asked what was bugging him. The mental tug of war took its toll on Grant. His already overwhelming ambivalence about his career had progressed rapidly to a feeling of captivity and a compulsion to flee.

Deep in thought late on a Thursday evening, Grant sat in his empty office on a simple folding chair behind a portable plastic table. No files, papers, or notebooks covered its surface. When he looked up he saw Charlie Montgomery leaning against the doorframe.

"Anything else you need?" Charlie asked.

"No, thanks. Just about done."

Montgomery stepped into the room with two glasses half filled with Crown Royal, a few ice cubes floating on the golden surface of each.

"Pull up a chair." Grant waved at the empty floor around him.

Charlie looked around and chuckled. "I'll stand, thanks." He handed Grant a glass and extended his. "Here's to you, Grant. You've been a fine partner. You're the best natural talent in the courtroom I ever saw. We'll miss you."

Each man took a swallow of the whiskey before Charlie spoke again.

"What's next for you?"

"I'm not coming back to the practice of law, at least not anytime soon," Grant said. "I think I'll take a sabbatical."

"How long?"

"I don't know," mused Grant. "Maybe a few months. Maybe the rest of my life."

"What does Samantha think?"

"It'll present some challenges," he said with a hollow laugh. "There'll be some belt tightening, and she'll need to find a job. We'll probably put the lake house up for sale."

Charlie sighed. "You have some cash stowed away, don't you?"

"Enough to last awhile, I think." Grant nodded.

The two men remained silent for a moment, each taking another sip of whiskey.

"You scared?" Montgomery asked.

Grant stared out the window. "Sure I am. Who wouldn't be? But as much as unemployment scares me, it's not nearly as terrifying as the thought of doing this."

"You just went through a pretty tough experience with the Haller case," Charlie said. "Maybe you just need a few weeks off to recharge."

"I thought about that. No doubt the stuff with the Hallers took it out of me." Only Grant knew the whole truth about the Haller matter, and he alone understood the full effect. "The whole thing is such a tragedy. But that's not all. You know I've never liked this. I've been at it more than twenty years now, and I just can't do it anymore. I'm cooked, Charlie."

In truth, the practice had robbed Grant of hope and optimism. As the years went by, he'd started to see the world in terms of antagonism and adversarial settings. "You know, Charlie, once the love of conflict evaporates, it's time for a litigator to find another way to make a living."

"You're probably right," Montgomery said, finishing his drink. "You ready to go?"

"Not yet. You go ahead, though."

Montgomery raised his glass again. "Don't be a stranger."

Grant sat in his chair, nursing the Crown Royal as he looked out the window and pondered his next step. As his children had grown, he reminded them as often as possible of a saying he'd learned from his mother. She'd told Grant that life isn't measured by the number of breaths taken, but by the moments that take your breath away. Grant hoped with all his heart he'd soon find a true calling, a career in which he could do things that would take his breath away, at least every now and then. He figured he'd find it, but was pretty sure it wouldn't involve filing lawsuits, taking depositions, and crossing swords with lawyers.

He knew he'd miss parts of it. The money was a warm blanket of reassurance in a time when many people were simply thankful for a job and lived in daily fear of losing what they had. Being a lawyer had occasionally provided light moments and had given him the opportunity to represent many fine people. He'd helped run a successful firm with an outstanding partner and had gained the admiration and respect of opponents and colleagues. Overall, Grant was proud of his career, the relationships he'd built, and the job he'd done. He just knew it was time to go.

These thoughts were with Grant as he stood in the door of his office, the last box under his arm. He switched off the light and stood alone in the darkness, admiring the view out his window. Below, Fort Worth's city lights twinkled as they stretched toward Dallas, the headlights and taillights of the ever-present traffic reminding him that life goes on.

With a deep breath, he turned, walked down the hall, and rode the elevator to the lobby. Grant Mercer grabbed his box, walked out the front door of the building, and climbed into the Tahoe. He pointed the truck to the west and drove.

# ACKNOWLEDGMENTS

In my experience, and I would imagine in most, writing a book is anything but a solitary venture. It begins long before pen is ever put to paper, born of love for reading and writing, and flourishes thanks to the influence of others.

For me, it began with my big sister Patty, who decided that the best way to pass the time during a hot summer in El Paso, Texas, was to play school. She was the teacher, of course, and I was her student. As with most teachers, she expected me to read my assignments every day and to report to her on my reading. The only trouble with this plan was that I was only four years old at the time and couldn't read. Never easily dissuaded, Patty simply ignored my objections and proceeded to teach me. Within weeks, I was reading books intended for third and fourth graders. My life would never have been the same if not for that one hot summer.

My parents were delighted that Patty had forbidden TV watching during that summer, and continued to feed me books. Throughout my childhood and into college, my constant memory is of my parents reading and passing down their favorites to me. My Dad still reads several dozen books each year, and my Mom belongs to a couple of book clubs. Parents should never underestimate the power of books and their own love for books on their children. I know mine never did.

Thanks to my wife Sherri and my daughters, Ashley and Kelley, for giving me encouragement during the writing and re-writing. Thanks to my sister Theresa for her feedback and for checking on my amateur medical opinions. Any errors on that front are mine alone. Thanks to my friends and fellow attorneys Terry Turzinski and Bill Mateja, each of whom brought unique professional perspective to the legal aspects of the book. To all my friends and family who have read the book, liked it, and kept up with this rollercoaster ride, I can't thank you enough.

Lynn Calvert deserves credit for taking a chance on an unpublished novelist, as does Jocelyn Kelley for her work promoting the book. Many thanks to my labelmates at Otherworld Richard Thomas, Laura Griffith, and Tom Matthews for their relentless promotion of me and my book. Thanks to my fellow authors Chris Reich, Mark Engebretson, Ian Graham, Bill Evans, Larry Groebel and Dennis Welch for their endorsements and encouragement, and to the countless others who gave of themselves without hesitation and without expectation of anything in return.

I especially owe Linda Green for providing the final push. Linda is the one who put me up to this in the first place. After enduring four years of my incessant threats to actually write a book, Linda challenged me, for my birthday, to participate in National Novel Writing Month, where the idea is to write a 50,000-word first draft of a novel in 30 days. As she pointed out to me at the time, it was a gift, and it would have been rude to decline. I may have received some gifts over the years that I liked better, but none was ever more important.

Also from
OTHERWORLD PUBLICATIONS

# Otherworld Publications
Let's Form The Future Together

## *TRANSUBSTANTUATE* by Richard Thomas

"They say Jimmy made it out. But the postcards we get, well, they don't seem...real."
     When an experiment with population control works too well, and the planet is decimated, seven broken people are united by a supernatural bond in a modern day Eden. Most on the island are fully aware of this prison disguised as an oasis. Unfortunately, Jimmy is on the mainland, desperate to get back, in a post-apocalyptic stand-off, fighting for his survival and that of his unborn child. Back on the island, Jacob stares at the ocean through his telescope and plots his escape, reluctant to aid the cause. Marcy tries to hide from her past sexual escapades that may be her saving grace. X sits in his compound, a quiet, massive presence, trapped in his body by ancient whispers and yet free in spirit to visit other places and times. Roland, the angry, bitter son of Marcy is determined to leave, and sets out on his own. Watching over it all is Assigned, the ghost in the machine. And coming for them, to exact revenge, and finish the job that the virus started, is Gordon. He just landed on the island and he has help.

     *Transubstantiate* is a neo-noir thriller, filled with uncertainty at every portal, and jungles infiltrated with The Darkness. Vivid settings, lyrical language, and a slow reveal of plot, motivation, past crimes and future hope collide in a showdown that keeps you guessing until the final haunting words.

Transubstantiate: to change from one substance into another.

## The Silk Worm by David Rosenstein

CIA agent, Richard Gibson, is sent to Hong Kong where he is to meet with a known informant to assess the possibility that a major assault of cyber terrorism, the next terrorism, is about to be unleashed on the free world by brilliant Chinese graduate student, Lee Yong, in an attempt to remove the evil influence of western values imposed upon his country by the capitalist countries of the world.

Richard assembles a team of America's top computer experts to try and thwart the attack. Within days of Richard's team starting to work out possible scenarios, the first attack of the Silk Worm hits an airport control tower in northern Taiwan, which results in the crash of two airliners and the death of over three hundred and fifty passengers. The American Ambassador in China is instructed by the President of the United States to lobby the Chinese government in an attempt to allow this team to setup shop in Hong Kong to lead and work with Chinese agents in an effort to kill the attacking computer program and capture its creator. Richard and his group of field agents hit the streets of Hong Kong with telemetry coordinates in hand to search for the physical locations of the ones responsible for the attack and soon discover that they are the ones being hunted.

## *The Oracle: The Succession War* by Richard Wayne Waterman

What price would you be willing to pay for an instrument of absolute power? Would you be willing to betray your friends and family, to even kill your own father? Or would you be willing to commit even more heinous acts of mass murder, including genocide?

Guided by the spirit of a dark and powerful villain, the demented Count Belicki, various vibrantly articulated characters discover that they must sacrifice something they treasure more than life itself in order to acquire the transcendent power of the mysterious Oracle. Driven by an insatiable ambition, these individuals seek unlimited power, for if they are strong enough to bend the Oracle to their own will; it is capable of translating mere thoughts into stark reality.

But these mere humans are not the only ones who seek to control the Oracle. For the battle for omnipotence also occurs within the Oracle itself.

### *Stay God* by Nik Korpon

Damon lives a content life, playing video games and dealing drugs from his second-hand store while his girlfriend, Mary, drops constant hints about marriage. If only he could tell her his name isn't really Damon. If only he could tell her who he really is. But after he witnesses a friend's murder, a scarlet woman glides into his life, offering the solution to all of his problems. His carefully constructed existence soon shatters like crystal teardrops and he must determine which ghosts won't stay buried—and which ones are trying to kill him—if he wants to learn why Mary has disappeared.

## *Remember* by Laura Griffith

After a freak car accident, Professor Robert Madigan begins to suffer impairment of his short-term memory. Suddenly, moments that have just occurred are impossible for him to recall. His family and friends struggle to help him, but, as time goes by, it starts to appear to be more than a temporary condition. His job, his marriage, and his life begin to suffer, but nothing he tries to do works.

On his way home from work one evening, Robert finds himself standing over a battered, dead body. His hands are covered in blood. He has no recollection of what transpired before that very moment. The police arrive on the scene and take the professor in for questioning as their lead suspect.

As the police investigate the murder and sort out the details, Robert and his family begin to question the professor's lost memory. Had he been under enough stress to snap? Or did he witness a crime that he cannot remember the details of? And if he were a witness, what would a murderer do to keep his only witness quiet?

To uncover the truth, Robert must work with the detectives to piece together what happened that evening, no matter what the cost. But will he remember anything, and will it be too late?

THE PRICE OF LIFE

"Hurts, doesn't it?" asked the man, leaning close to Purser's face.

"What the hell is this about?" Purser stammered between labored breaths. "If it's money you want, tell me how much. I'll get it."

Knobs were spun again, this time delivering voltage to Purser's groin and feet. Purser screamed as the agony continued for thirty seconds, at which time the man calmly returned the dials to zero.

Purser's brow beaded with sweat, and his breath came in short, ragged bursts. "Please stop," he cried. "I'll give you whatever you want, I promise."

"There's nothing I want from you," the man replied as he turned the controls for the leads attached to the man's nipples and groin once more. The indicators on the dials spun to eight on their scale of ten.

Purser screamed again. The smell of burning flesh filled the room.

"No more," he pleaded over and over again.

"Maybe this will feel better," said the man as he turned off the current and lifted his scalpel.

He felt scant resistance as the knife entered Purser's skin, circling the clip attached to his nipple and excising the flesh cleanly. He held the chunk of tissue in front of Purser's eyes as it swayed hypnotically back and forth on thin strands of wire. After a momentary pause, pain signals reached Purser's brain and the screaming began for real.

"No?" asked the man, feigning concern. "Sorry about that. I thought you said the electricity hurt."

After a minute or so, Purser's shrieking became less fervent, replaced by labored breathing and gentle sobbing. He tried to talk, but was unable to form words. As soon as Purser started to speak, the

LaVergne, TN USA
10 September 2010

196516LV00002BA/3/P